TALES OF THE DARK FOREST

TALES OF THE DARK FOREST

WHIZZARD!

STEVE BARLOW & STEVE SKIDMORE

ILLUSTRATED BY FIONA LAND

Collins
VOYAGER

An imprint of HarperCollinsPublishers

First published in Great Britain by Collins Voyager in 2002
Collins Voyager is an imprint of HarperCollins*Publishers* Ltd,
77-85 Fulham Palace Road, Hammersmith,
London, W6 8JB

5 7 9 8 6 4

Text copyright © Steve Barlow and Steve Skidmore 2002
Illustrations by Fiona Land 2002

ISBN 0 00 710864 8

The authors and illustrator assert the moral right to
be identified as the authors and illustrator of the work.

Printed and bound in England by
Clays Ltd, St Ives plc

The Legend of the Dark Forest

According to legend, the Dark Forest was not always dark. Long ago, the Kings of the Forest ruled a rich and fertile land from their high throne in the great City of Dun Indewood. Their prosperous and peaceful realm was defended by brave and honourable Knyghts, and you couldn't throw a rock without hitting a beautiful maiden, a sturdy forester or a rosy, apple-cheeked farmer. (Of course, none of the contented citizens of Dun Indewood would ever dream of throwing rocks about anyway; and if they did, one of the Knyghts, who were not only brave and honourable but just and kindly too, would ask them very politely not to do it again.)

It was a Golden Age.

But over the years, the Knyghts and Lords of the City grew greedy, idle and dishonest, and fell to quarrelling among themselves. The line of the Kings died out.

The power of Dun Indewood declined. Contact with the other cities and towns that lay in the vast wilderness of the Dark Forest became rare, and then was lost altogether when the Forest roads became too dangerous to travel.

The creatures of the Forest became wild and dangerous until only a few hardy souls dared to brave its perils. The citizens of Dun Indewood continued to argue among themselves and cheat each other, turning their backs on everything that happened outside the City walls.

With no one to tame it, the Forest became home to truly dreadful things. Beasts with the understanding of men, and men with the ferocity of beasts, roamed the dark paths. The trees themselves became malevolent and watchful. And the Forest grew...

Well, that's the legend, anyway.

Of course, these days, nobody believes a word of it...

CHAPTER ONE

How Tym became a Wizard's Apprentice and went to Sleep on the Job.

"Take a card. Any card." Tym fanned out the deck of cards in his right hand and held them out invitingly. The audience member he had chosen gave him a suspicious, sidelong look from one beady eye.

"Yes, madam, any card. Don't let me see it." The 'volunteer' made a nervous, darting movement and snatched a single card.

"Good. Take a good look at it. Make sure you remember it. Now, put the card back in the pack." The volunteer looked bewildered. "All right, I'll put it back in the pack. Now shuffle…" Tym gave a resigned sigh, "I mean, *I'll* shuffle the pack. I will now tap the pack with my finger three times, and behold! A card is rising from the pack! Yes, here it comes! Madam, this card, the Four of Acorns, was the very card you chose!"

Tym's audience completely failed to burst into astonished and ecstatic applause. Its members stared stonily at Tym, before ignoring him completely and pecking at stray bits of grain.

Tym sighed again. It wasn't much fun doing card tricks for chickens. It was hard to persuade them to take a card even when you held it right under their beaks, and when they did take one they usually tried to eat it. And they hardly ever remembered which card they had chosen.

"Tym!"

Tym ignored the call and settled down in the hay. He folded his hands behind his head with a self-satisfied smile.

"Tym!" His mother's voice was shrill with anger. "There's work to be done! Where are you, you lazy rapscallion?"

Tym wriggled his feet luxuriously in the tickly straw. It had taken him ages to construct this hiding place at the back of the hayloft, but it was a good one. His mother hadn't found him in a week.

"You'll be sorry when I get my hands on you, you useless, born-tired, work-shy slubberdegullion!"

Tym grinned to himself. He was an expert at doing nothing. He put a lot of effort into it. It had taken years of dedicated study to learn the art of Never Being Around When He Was Wanted.

"Layabout!" screeched his mother, her voice fading as she walked off in the wrong direction. "Do-nothing! Slug-a-bed!"

It wasn't that Tym minded work, as long as someone else was doing it. But in his opinion, menial farm chores were not suitable employment for someone whose destiny was to be a famous wizard. And this was Tym's destiny; or would be, but for an accident of birth.

Tym's brow furrowed as he considered his problem for the umpteen-hundredth time. Traditionally, you could only become a wizard if you were the seventh son of a seventh son, which Tym wasn't. He was only the first son of a second son, and that didn't amount to much, even when you multiplied it. Nor was he likely to have any more brothers since his father had industriously dug a bearpit out in the Forest, then carelessly forgotten where it was and fallen into it. Unhappily, there had been a bear trapped in it at the time.

Tym had thought his troubles were over when the village wizard, Herbit the Potions Master, had advertised for an assistant on a Warlock Placement Scheme. On his first day, Tym had even turned up for work on time, eager to learn the secrets and mysteries of the sorcerer's craft. Herbit had scowled at him.

Tym had tried a charm offensive (though not the magical kind). "Thank you for giving me the job, Master," he had said with an ingratiating smile. "I know how lucky I am that you chose me as your assistant."

Herbit had grunted. "Not really. You were the only applicant."

"Oh." Tym's smile had slipped a bit. "What will my duties be, Master?"

Herbit considered. "I suppose you will be my factotum."

Tym brightened up. This sounded promising. "What does that mean, Master?"

"You see those two big buckets over there? They are real? They are not an illusion? They are, in short, fact?"

"Oh, yes, Master."

"Good. Then you can tote 'em!" And with a terrific kick to the seat of Tym's britches, the Potions Master had set him to work fetching and carrying water from the well and firewood from the Forest. His other duties involved sweeping, dusting and tidying the wizard's workshop, and watching the potions to make sure they didn't boil over as they gurgled, glopped and bubbled on the fire. Under Herbit's direction, Tym had learned a lot about housework, pounding herbs, washing out cauldrons and keeping fires burning at the right temperature. About magic, he had learned nothing at all.

A shaft of sunlight fell through a knothole and shone into Tym's eyes. He groaned. Time to go to work for Herbit. But at least he'd managed to avoid the morning chores for his mother. Tym grinned, slipped out of the hayloft and set off down the winding Forest path that led from the village of Leafy Bottom to Herbit's workshop.

"What time do you call this!" Wizard Herbit, standing at the door of his workshop, gave Tym his customary greeting. "You're late, crosswort!" (The Potions Master had a habit of using the names of herbs as curse-words.) Herbit glared at Tym. "I'm going to have to dock your wages."

Tym considered pointing out that this was technically impossible as Herbit didn't pay him any wages, but he decided against it. Among Herbit's potions were some that could make you feel as if your belly were full of snakes or your veins full of ants: there was one, to Tym's certain knowledge, that could make steam come whistling out of your ears. Tym didn't want to be on the wrong end of one of Herbit's brews!

The wizard gave Tym a cuff on the back of the head as he stooped to enter through the low doorway. "Now you're here, dodder, you can light the fire and sweep the floors." The wizard shouldered a bag and scowled. "And see you do it properly! No sweeping dust under the bench this time, mind! I'm going into the Forest to pay a visit to my colleague, Bertole the Weather Monger."

Tym breathed a sigh of relief. At least that would keep the cross-grained wizard out of his way for the rest of the day. Bertole lived in the neighbouring village of Mulch Hemlock. On his visits to his fellow wizard, Herbit always took along a bottle of something he made in a private still that Tym wasn't allowed to touch, and he and Bertole would stay up late into the night boasting about their latest spells, singing rude songs and giggling.

Herbit swung round in the doorway and pointed sternly at

Tym. "And when I come back, I want to be able to eat my dinner off the floor!" Tym made a non-committal noise. The Potions Master always wanted to eat his dinner off the floor when he returned from the Forest. This seemed a strange ambition to Tym: what was wrong with plates, for goodness' sake?

Herbit strode off. Tym stepped inside the workshop, peering around, waiting for his eyes to adjust to the gloom.

The Potions Master's workshop was a long, low, single-roomed dwelling with wattle-and-daub walls and a thatched roof. The roof timbers and the thatch were blackened with soot from generations of fires, and the smell of smoke hung heavily on the stale air.

Jars clustered on shelves around the walls. They were filled with horrible yellow things floating in glutinous liquids, and bore peeling labels in Wizard Herbit's best handwriting. Unfortunately, Wizard Herbit's best handwriting was practically illegible. Tym could only make out a few names of the gruesome ingredients:

Livere of Beare
Lunges of ye Wilde Boare
Spleene of Cameleoparde
Fishe Featherse
Essence of Mouse Droppynges
Tonsilse of Hagge
Ogeres Toenailse
Badger spitte

Some of the labels were even more baffling:

Squiggle of donkey's loopy curly splodge
Blotch of black line's bottom
Scrawl of bats something
Blot of cross-out netherdrawers

Some of the bottles contained concocted mixtures:

A Potione to cure ye Wartes
A Potione to relieve ye Bloate in Sheepe
A Potione to mayke yrself Irresistible to Ladies

(This last label was crossed out with a note below it: *Doesn't worke.*)

A Potione to cure Bruises and Bumps caused bye ladies...

Above these grisly exhibits, stuffed birds hung forlornly from wires fixed to the beams, swinging uneasily in the fitful draughts from the ill-fitting door and windows in a grotesque parody of flight. Under one particularly sooty beam was suspended a small, stuffed dragon with a moulting tail and a very fed-up expression. Its name was Algernon.

At one end of the building, a partition divided off Herbit's bedroom – or "Cell" as the wizard insisted on calling it. Tym would have preferred to see Herbit in a different sort of cell – one with iron bars and chains – but this was another thought he had never voiced aloud. Tym wasn't allowed in Herbit's Cell. He couldn't imagine why – there was nothing there except a fireplace that never had a fire in it, a rickety old bed with a chamber pot underneath it, and an even more rickety chair. Herbit set little store by creature comforts.

The rest of the building was the Potions Master's workshop. In its centre was a long bench covered with chopping boards, mortars and pestles, and various bowls for mixing potions. At the end opposite the Cell was a huge fireplace with an iron framework above it. A number of hooks hung from this structure. Several of these were occupied by cauldrons containing the mixture to be brewed that day.

Tym sighed again and slouched over to the woodpile beside the fireplace. He carefully laid a fire on the hearth and scraped a spark from his tinderbox. When the fire was well alight, he swung the largest cauldron over it and waited for the mixture to boil.

It was on this hearth that Herbit distilled his potions, concocted from the plants of the Dark Forest and other ingredients he stubbornly refused to talk about. All he would tell Tym, in answer to his servant's questions, was that for his potions it was necessary to extract the vital essence from each ingredient. Herbit clearly had no intention of sharing the secret of what this 'essence' might be. Tym decided it must be the 'heart' or 'life force' of the substance, bearing its mystical qualities.

"The lore of potions demands years of arcane research, decades of experimentation, generations of study," the wizard would declaim when Tym's questioning became too insistent. "Are you prepared for that?"

Of course, Tym wasn't. It sounded like too much hard work. But he said, "Teach me, Master."

And then the Wizard Herbit would shake his head. "All in good time. You must show me that you are prepared to learn. After all my years of research, I am still learning."

At these moment's Tym's mind would seethe with silent scorn. Herbit was an old man: what did he know? Tym was the future. He was young. He could do anything, be anything. He would be the greatest wizard in the Dark Forest! ...one day.

One day.

Tym sighed yet again and did a bit of listless sweeping up (brushing the dust under Herbit's workbench as usual). Then he sat down to watch the potion which was now bubbling away merrily in its cauldron. As the heat of the fire and the warmth of the day spread through him, Tym's eyes closed. His head drooped. His breathing became deep and regular. He began to snore.

Tym lay on a day-bed crafted from pure silver and upholstered in cloth-of-gold. He graciously accepted a grape that a serving-maiden had just peeled for him. Another serving-maiden was fanning him with soft feathers, while a third offered him a glass of cocoa. (It always bothered Tym that in his dreams the only drink he was ever offered was cocoa. He felt it ought to be sherbert, but as far as he knew, sherbert was that powdery stuff that got up your nose. He had no idea how you made a drink from it or what it would taste like if you did, so his dreaming imagination had to settle for cocoa.)

Wizard Herbit came shuffling in on his knees, sobbing with remorse, to beg Tym's pardon for treating him so harshly. Tym graciously turned Herbit into a newt. The other wizards in the room – who were standing around anxiously clutching things like slippers or mirrors in case Tym should suddenly feel the need for them – burst into enthusiastic (if somewhat frightened) applause.

Feeling peckish, Tym created a banquet: roast peacock decorated with the tail feathers, sizzling wild boar sausages and venison cutlets followed by sticky toffee pudding and custard, and to drink... some more cocoa. Tym wrinkled his nose in his sleep and made a mental note to have a word with his imagination.

Tym's dreams always went something like this. Ordinary people in his village laboured relentlessly from dawn to sunset every day – and for what? A mud hut to live in, rags to sleep on, some gritty bread and woody vegetables for supper, and a few scraps of gristle on Songday – if they were lucky.

When Tym became a wizard, he wouldn't have to work. He'd be able to magic anything he wanted! Nobody would be able to push him around any more. He would be powerful. People would do what he said! Tym was willing to put up with his cantankerous master for as long as it took to gain that reward. Because when Tym became a wizard, he would be living in a palace – and Herbit would be living in a pond.

Tym smiled in his sleep.

But then his dream changed. The palace and wizards and banquet disappeared. Tym frowned, whimpering a little. This had never happened before. What was going on? He wanted the nice dream to come back.

But it didn't. Instead, Tym was alone on a vast, desolate plain. He squinted into the expanse of barren wasteland, but could see nothing. The ground was flat and featureless. Above the brooding wilderness, the sky was starless and black. A biting wind sprang up and skewered his body. He began to shake. As he peered into the awesome void, a dark shape formed in the air before him.

Tym gave a cry of alarm. The shape had taken on a human form, but one made of darkness and shadows. The great figure swept across half the sky. In a face as sombre as the night, two bright stars glittered for eyes. Tym gazed up at the huge creature in wonder.

"*Have no fear, boy,*" The voice was deep and commanding. "*I am not here to harm you.*"

Tym was only partly comforted by this reassurance. "*Where am I?*" he stammered.

"*In my world,*" replied the figure. "*The world of dreams, where you have sought me out.*"

"*Who are you?* "

The figure spread its arms. "*I am the Dreamwalker.*"

CHAPTER TWO

How Tym met the Dreamwalker, and how his Spelling brought Tears to his Eyes.

The Dreamwalker's outstretched arms seemed to cover the plain from edge to edge. Tym gazed up at the huge creature, trembling with fear.

"Are you real," he asked, *"or are you just a dream?"*

"I am as real as your dreams," replied the Dreamwalker. *"Do you not wish that your dreams should come true?"*

"But dreams only happen when people are asleep," protested Tym. *"I'm asleep now, so I'm dreaming you, but when I wake up you'll be gone. Nothing I dream is real."*

"You think not? You must dare to dream, boy," whispered the dark mass in the voice of the night wind. *"All men must. For*

many years, the people of the Dark Forest have been afraid to dream, and I have been... absent. But now a new hope is stirring and my time is come again. Now, at last, men need me..." It regarded Tym with eyes that shone with the harsh glitter of countless stars. *"As I, in my turn, need men."*

"Yes, but how can I believe in a dream?" Tym demanded. *"How can I believe in you?"*

"Do you really wish to know the power of dreams?"

"It's all very well talking about power," said Tym pettishly, *"but how do I... Aaargghhhh!"*

In the blink of an eye, the ground beneath Tym's feet had crumbled away. There was nothing below him, only sky. Tym screamed as he plummeted down, the air whistling around his body. Below, the ground was getting nearer and nearer with every racing heartbeat. *"Heeeeelp!"*

Just before Tym slammed into it, the ground vanished. His scream was cut off as he plunged into black, freezing water. Down he plunged, down, down... and invisible, clinging tentacles wrapped themselves around his body, drawing him into a loathsome, rubbery embrace while his lungs cried out for air. He kicked and twisted, but he couldn't break free of the sinewy grip. He was going to drown.

"You are real!" Water poured into Tym's lungs as he appealed to the Dreamwalker. *"I believe you! I belie... beli... bel... be... b..."* It was too late; Tym felt himself slipping away.

"Good!"

Tym gave a start. He was back on the plain, completely dry. The Dreamwalker stood before him once again. Tym shook with relief and gasped in the acrid air.

"*Believe in your dreams,*" said the Dreamwalker sternly. "*Without dreams, there are only nightmares. All beings must have dreams, desires and hope. Without them, how can they survive the disappointment and sadness of the waking world? Dreams have no price. Riches cannot buy them. The beggar dreams of a better life, the prisoner of freedom. The king dreams of power, but having achieved it, he dreams of the enemies he slew to gain his throne. He cannot choose. All need their dreams and I decree what those dreams shall be.*" It paused before adding pointedly, "*There are some who dream of being greater than their masters.*"

Tym took the hint. "*Do you mean that my dreams will come true?*"

"*It is not in my power to tell you what the future holds. What you dream in my world and what will take place in your world may not be the same.*" The Dreamwalker's voice was thoughtful. "*You dream of being a great wizard, do you not, boy?*"

Speechless, Tym nodded.

"*Yet you know that there are many years of work and study along that road, and much peril. You seek an easier way.*"

Tym could not meet the Dreamwalker's eyes.

"*Perhaps I can help you.*" Tym looked up, eyes wide with hope: but the Dreamwalker shook its great head. "*With my aid, you can become something great. I can help you to achieve a remarkable power. But if I do, you must use it wisely and be guided by me.*"

"*Oh, I will!*" promised Tym. "*But what must I do to gain this power?*"

The Dreamwalker made a gesture in the air. Something white fluttered out of the black sky to land at Tym's feet. It was a small piece of parchment. Tym picked it up.

"Farewell." Tym looked up again as the Dreamwalker raised its great right hand in a gesture of parting. *"You have my gift. Use it well. And remember,"* the voice continued, *"always follow your dreams. Only be true to your true self and you will gain your heart's desire."*

Tym awoke with a jerk. The mixture in the cauldron had almost boiled dry. Cursing, Tym pulled it off the heat – then gave a shriek of pain and hopped about, blowing on his scorched fingers. He stuffed them into his mouth. At the same moment, he realised that he was holding something in his left hand. Something flat and crinkly.

The pain of his burnt fingers forgotten, Tym stared in disbelief at the parchment he was holding. His dream came flooding back to him. The Dreamwalker! In his dream, the shadowy figure had given him a parchment – and here it was! How was that *possible*?

Then Tym shrugged. Magic *wasn't* possible: that was what made it magic.

He examined the parchment closely. It seemed to be a recipe.

Take thou yee esensse of ye Erthe

Mixe welle with ye essinee of ye Wattere

Infewse wyth yee esssenee of ye Aire

Boyle for anne houre uponne ye fyre of ye dryed skinnes
of ye Salmandere

Adde three droppes of thyne owne Bloode

Allowe to coole. Adde Sugere to taste.

Serve chillede wythe ye slyce of Lemone (optionale)

As recipes went, it seemed easy enough. The trouble was, Tym had no idea how to get started. What on Earth was 'essence of Air'? What in the Air was 'essence of Earth'? Tym had been through all Herbit's grubby bottles, and every phial in his phialing cabinet, and he'd never found any such potions, although there was definitely a whole jarful of salamander skins on the mantelpiece.

But the Dreamwalker wouldn't have given Tym the recipe if the ingredients were impossible to obtain. Perhaps Herbit had hidden them somewhere? Tym considered this carefully.

If I were Herbit, he thought, and I wanted to hide something where I (Tym) couldn't find it, where would I (Herbit) put it? And the answer came to him: I (Herbit) would hide it where I (Tym) would know it couldn't possibly be. And just for good measure, I (Herbit) would forbid me (Tym) to go in there.

So Tym went and searched Herbit's Cell. He checked that there was nothing hidden in the wizard's bed (a feat of some daring in itself). Then, screwing up his courage, he looked in Herbit's chamber pot. When he'd recovered from this experience he tried the fireplace. Several sooty minutes later he discovered the tin box Herbit had hidden on a ledge halfway up the chimney and bore it back to the workshop in triumph.

The lid of the box was covered with an inscription warning about the things that would happen to a thief who opened the box. These were all fatal in extremely unpleasant ways. Tym decided to ignore them. After all, he wasn't a thief. He worked for Herbit. That meant he was allowed to use the wizard's potions. Herbit hadn't actually said that Tym wasn't allowed to use the potions in the tin box because he'd never told Tym that the tin box existed. So that was all right then.

Hardly daring to breathe, Tym cautiously inched open the lid. You never knew what you might find in a box belonging to a wizard. To Tym's relief, nothing nasty jumped out at him and no booby trap spell was activated to turn him into a frog. The box simply contained a number of phials including, to his delight, all the puzzling ingredients for the Dreamwalker's recipe.

Eagerly, Tym set to work – grinding up the essence of Earth (which was crumbly and dark brown shot through with glittering specks of crystals) and mixing it with essence of Water (which was, unexpectedly, rather syrupy and a bluey-pink colour). He guessed that the phial containing essence of Air held gas under pressure, so he built an apparatus to bubble it through the essences of Earth and Water. The phial seemed to contain a lot of gas for its size: probably due to magic, Tym decided.

When the essence of Air had stopped bubbling, the resulting potion looked like some kind of soup – possibly the primordial soup from which, according to some wizards at the cutting edge of Theoretical Magic, all life was supposed to have sprung. Tym couldn't imagine any sort of life springing from this soup, except possibly his Uncle Erny, who (his mother insisted) "We Don't Talk About".

Tym set to work assembling Herbit's distillation equipment (which was known in wizarding jargon as an alembic) and poured the elemental soup into a glass vessel with a long spout (a retort). He placed this over the fire to warm up while he shredded salamander skins. He'd almost finished this task when he heard a sound that turned his blood to lumpy gravy.

"Great news! Great news! Ohohohohoho!"

Tym's stomach did a backflip as the wizard's voice echoed round the glade outside. Herbit never came back this early! What had happened? Hastily, Tym grabbed Herbit's tin box and flung it under the bench. Then he snatched the retort from the flames, wrapped it in a rag – and stuffed it down his britches just as Herbit came in through the door.

"Master," gasped Tym. "I thought you were visiting Wizard Bertole!"

The Potions Master was grinning like a gargoyle. "I was – but I met a messenger from the City of Dun Indewood on the way. Congratulate me, my boy!"

Tym gave a little moan. The retort was hot! He surreptitiously fanned at the front of his britches with one hand and gritted his teeth. "Why, Master?"

"Recognition, lad! And not before time!" Herbit held up a roll of parchment with a seal in the colours of the High Lord of the City. "I have been invited to the WOSCAS!"

Tym was now hopping from foot to foot, flapping with both hands and pouring with sweat. "The what, Master?"

Herbit's face settled into something more like his usual discontented expression. "WOSCAS, mugwort! The Wizards' Order for Spells, Charms And Sorcery. In times gone by, all the wizards of the Dark Forest met in Dun Indewood and awards were given to those who had made the greatest contribution to magic. Those were the WOSCAS. Of course, they weren't held in the High Lord Gordin's time. He didn't like wizards. But now he's gone, High Lord Robat has directed the Chief Wizard of Dun Indewood to reinstate them. The first round of the competition will be held in a few days."

For the first time, Herbit noticed Tym's strange, sweaty cavortings. "Why are you dancing like that, boy? What ails you? You look like a frog in a furnace."

Tym was now bent almost double and blowing frantically downwards. The rag was unwrapping itself from round the retort, and what Tym's mother referred to as his "bits-down-there" were on the verge of spontaneous combustion. "Just a touch of plague, I think, Master. I've taken some potion for it. I'll be all right soon."

"Very well. Mend that fire then – it's high time I got to work!"

Tym gazed at his employer with horror. Herbit was distracted with glee, but as soon as he calmed down he was bound to notice the mess in his workshop – and Tym's britches were starting to smoulder. "Now, Master? What about Wizard Bertole?"

"I haven't time to go visiting that old fraud! I must prepare. No time like the present. I'm going to win WOSCAS for my potions if it's the last thing I do!"

Tym bit back a scream of despair. "But, Master, surely you wish to share the news of your good fortune with your friend?"

Herbit looked up with a stunned expression. "Marry, lad, well bethought!" His face took on an unpleasant leer. "Perchance the old goat hasn't been invited. Then we'll see who is the more powerful wizard. As if any fool couldn't conjure up a thunderstorm…"

"I should go now if I were you, Master," bleated Tym, fearing that bits of him were about to melt and run like treacle. "So he hears the news from you and no one else."

"Good counsel!" Herbit gave Tym a hearty slap on the back that unwound the rag around the retort a little more. "You show sound judgement – for a pettimuggett!" With another bellow of laughter, and waving his invitation like a flag, Herbit strode out of the workshop.

With a gasp, Tym dragged the seething retort from its hiding place and rushed to the water-butt. He dropped a ladleful of cold water down the inside of his britches… which steamed.

When Tym had cooled to normal operating temperature, he completed the Dreamwalker's recipe by distilling the mixture in the alembic. He sprinkled half the Potions Master's stock of salamander skins on the fire, where they burned with an even, deep red glow. He set the retort back on the heat, being careful not to allow it to boil too fiercely. He watched with bated breath as the steam crept through the network of pipes that slowly cooled it to liquid. He boiled the mixture for exactly one hour by Herbit's hourglass timer, as instructed. The distilled potion dripped slowly into a flask.

At last, all the mixture in the first flask had boiled away and the last drop of distilled potion had dripped into the collecting flask. There seemed to be quite a lot, so Tym poured about two thirds into a leather bottle, which he put aside for later use. He took the remaining third over to the workbench. There, he checked the Dreamwalker's recipe and gave a grimace of dismay. He had to let three drops of his own blood drip into the mixture. This was going to hurt!

At the third wincing attempt, Tym managed to jab his left thumb with a needle from Herbit's sewing kit. He carefully squeezed three drops of blood into the flask. As the third drop fell, there was a kind of soft explosion that sounded like *whup*! Lilac fumes formed and trickled over the mouth of the flask. The spell was complete. The potion was ready!

Still, Tym hesitated. He was meant to drink the potion. Could he trust the Dreamwalker not to poison him? It all seemed a bit risky to him.

Tym lived in a world of danger. The Dark Forest was a dangerous place. Quite apart from wolves, bears and wild boars, the Forest was home to outlaws and brigands as well as a host of magical, supernatural and just plain weird creatures that would eat Tym as soon as look at him. In Leafy Bottom, as in all the scattered villages that provided food and firewood for the neighbouring City of Dun Indewood, children were taught from their earliest years to stay away from the Forest. Every house, every barn and byre, every sty and stable was protected by stout doors and window shutters, and nobody left their home after dark. Woodsmen went armed and in threes. The convoys of farm produce that left every week for Dun Indewood were accompanied by a strong escort of archers and men-at-arms. And on his way to and from Herbit's workshop, Tym always kept an eye on the Forest and a dagger in his boot.

Was the potion safe or not? Tim had no idea how long the ingredients had been in Herbit's box. They were probably well past their spell-by date. And what was the potion supposed to do? The Dreamwalker hadn't told Tym, only that it would give him great power. But what sort of power? How badly did Tym want to find out? How badly did he want to be a wizard? To swig or not to swig?

"Hasn't been invited, ha!"

Tym spun round with a shriek of despair at the sound of the familiar voice. His Master had returned – and it was too late to tidy the workshop!

"That old fool Bertole got his invitation three weeks ago…" Herbit stopped dead in the open doorway and stared in horror at his plundered box. "What devilment is this? What are you doing with my box, you snooping sanguinaria?"

The wizard's face was white with fury. Any second now, he would snatch the potion away from Tym and beat him to within an inch of his life. It was now or never! Without thinking, Tym set the flask to his lips and swallowed.

"Viper's bugloss!" cried Herbit, pointing an accusing finger at Tym. He strode towards his apprentice who cringed, raising his arms to ward off the first blow. "You have defiled my Inner Sanctum." The wizard was trembling with rage. "Thief! Ingrate! Snakeweed! Fleawort! Scurvy…!"

Herbit suddenly stopped mid-rant. His eyes were wild and staring and his mouth wide open. From his throat there came a clicking noise, like the sound made by a cog turning a spit over a fire, but he made no other sound and didn't move a muscle.

Gradually, Tym uncringed. With great care, he stepped closer to Herbit, ready to bolt at any moment. With infinite caution, he reached out and gently prodded the wizard's arm. No reaction. Emboldened, Tym poked Herbit in the chest and tugged his beard. Nothing.

Tym walked all the way round the wizard. It didn't look as if there was anything wrong with the Potions Master: he'd just… stopped.

After a while, it became clear that Herbit wasn't going to move for the foreseeable future. With every hair on the back of his neck standing to attention, Tym backed out of the workshop and ran pell-mell back down the path to Leafy

Bottom. He erupted on to the village green… and skidded to a halt, heart pounding like a blacksmith's hammer.

The entire village was still. Not a man, not a woman, not a child moved. All stood like statues. Not a horse, not a cow, not a pig, sheep or goat twitched a muscle or made a sound. Not a leaf stirred. Birds hung motionless in the air. Smoke from cooking fires hung over the village as if painted on the sky.

Everything in the entire village was as stiff, still and silent as if it was carved out of stone.

CHAPTER THREE

How Tym left the villagers of Leafy Bottom
Quite Unmoved and Discovered the Secret
of changing Turnips into Gold.

Tym stared in stupefaction at his neighbours, caught out of
time in a moment from their everyday lives. Some had been
frozen mid-step and were balanced at impossible angles.
One of Tym's neighbours had been pouring the slops from
her washing over her vegetable patch, and the water hung
solidly between bucket and earth like ice. Her daughter had
been holding a rag doll by the leg and whirling it round her
head: the leg had come off and the body of the doll was
caught in the moment of breaking free, its arms flung wide in
motionless celebration.

Tym found his mother in mid-argument with her landlady,

an old enemy. His mother's face was twisted in anger, her mouth wide open to scold and one wagging finger stilled in front of the woman's nose.

"Mum!" Tym tugged at her sleeve. "Mum!"

Something had happened to his mother's dress. The homespun cloth felt just as it always had, but the folds made by Tym's clutching fingers did not fall out of the material. The creases remained, even after he had taken his hand away. And his mother gave no sign of having heard or seen him. In a panic, Tym jumped up and down, waving his arms in front of his mother's face.

"Mum!" he cried again. "Can you hear me? Can you see me? Mum! *Mum*!" But his mother never batted an eyelid. Tym backed away.

Wondering if he had somehow slipped back into the world of the Dreamwalker, he wandered around the village, through the silent, unmoving shapes of the people he knew.

"Hello!" he called. "Can anybody hear me?"

The only answer was a deathly hush. There were no human voices, no bird song, nothing but silence. Had the world come to an end, Tim wondered wildly? Surely he would have noticed! But everyone he had ever known was motionless – unseeing, unhearing. Tym had never felt so alone in his life. What was going on?

As he racked his brains for some clue, Tym glanced at one of the birds, wheeling above the village. Had it moved slightly? Tym watched the bird closely, hardly blinking. After what seemed several minutes, he realised that the creature's wings *had* moved from the bottom of their downstroke to the top of their upstroke, although he hadn't been able to follow their movement.

It was like the shadow on a sundial, Tym realised. You could watch it for ages and never see it move: nevertheless, it would creep imperceptibly across the dial, recording the passing hours. So that could mean...

Tym raced around the village again. Surely the water from his neighbour's bucket was closer to the ground than it had been? Surely her daughter's doll had flown further away from its detached leg...?

So... supposing the villagers hadn't stopped moving at all? Tym's brain cells whirred in his head. Supposing they were moving at normal speed? The difference between them and Tym was – that Tym had taken the Dreamwalker's potion! What if the potion was making him move more quickly than the villagers? So quickly that everyone else was almost completely still by comparison? Tym nodded slowly to himself. That would explain why the water was taking an age to splash on to the ground, why the doll was curving so slowly through the air. It also explained the strange clicks coming from Herbit's throat – what Tym had heard was the Potions Master's vocal cords vibrating!

Tym's mind was racing now. If this was true, it meant that he could walk as slowly as he liked and still go anywhere in the blink of an eye!

This was the Dreamwalker's gift! Thanks to the potion, Tym was moving faster than any human being who had ever lived.

He wasn't a wizard. He was a Whizzard!

Slowly, a sly grin spread over Tym's face. If he was moving so fast that the villagers of Leafy Bottom looked to him like statues, what did *he* look like to *them*? As long as he didn't stand still too long, the chances were that they wouldn't be able to see him at all! As far as the villagers were concerned, Tym was invisible!

He looked around and rubbed his hands together, chuckling. Then he set off for a stroll around the village, pulling faces at the villagers he didn't like, or who had scolded him in the past – which was most of them. Why not? Nobody could see him! He stuck his tongue out at everyone who had ever called him lazy and silly. Hah! Who was silly now? Tym wiggled his bottom at them.

He found Farmer Samwill, frozen in the act of leaping over a hurdle while his prize bull pounded behind him, caught mid-charge. As an experiment, Tym pushed the farmer – and was astonished and delighted to discover that he could move Samwill into any position he chose. Eventually, Tym settled for turning the farmer back to face his bull, with his tongue out and arms open wide.

Tym became bolder. He found the farmer's wife in the act of lowering her ample bottom on to a stool ready to milk her goat. Chortling, Tym took away the stool. Then he took away the goat.

Another of Tym's neighbours was thatching his roof. Tym removed his ladder.

Tym peered through windows. He helped himself from larders. He wandered into the Manor House. The Squire was the most important man in the village, but he was mean and never invited anyone to his house which was guarded by two fierce dogs. But now the dogs were frozen in mid-howl and the Squire, who was constantly telling his tenants they didn't work hard enough, was lazing in bed. Tym thought he looked lonely – so he fetched a pig to keep him company. It ought to have been very funny...

The trouble was, Tym realised, that although he could do anything he wanted to, he wasn't actually having much fun. There wasn't much point in playing tricks on people unless they *noticed*. Putting the pig in the bed wasn't the joke. The Squire waking up and *finding* the pig in his bed, that was the joke! But when would that happen? Half the fun of jokes was sharing them and Tym had no one to share them with.

Suddenly feeling miserable, Tym mooched out of the Manor House. He sat down on the edge of the horse-trough, and tried to think. Was he stuck in this motionless world for ever? Or could he learn to control this strange new power?

Tym closed his eyes and concentrated. He tried to relax. By degrees, he brought his breathing under control. Then he focused on his heartbeat. Slower, he told himself, running the word through his mind like a chant, over and over. Slow... slower... slowest...

In an instant, life returned to Leafy Bottom. Farmer Samwill found himself making faces at an infuriated bull. Moments later, he was flying though the air, landing with a crash on the roof of his hen house, which collapsed. His wife, trying to sit down on a stool that was no longer there, fell over backwards, flinging her bucket into the air. She landed with a thud, and looked around frantically for her goat. The roof-mender stepped off his roof on to the place where his ladder wasn't, and toppled backwards into a mud wallow with a shriek. And from the Squire's bedroom came the sound of infuriated roars and frantic squealing as both the Squire and the pig objected to his bedfellow.

Tym listened to the uproar and grinned to himself. How would the villagers explain their misfortunes? Then his grin disappeared. If he was now moving at the same speed as the villagers, he would be moving at the same speed as Herbit, too! Could he speed up again?

Fast... faster... fastest. Tym whizzed back to the workshop. He needn't have worried. Perhaps Herbit had moved forward a fraction (and he was certainly redder in the face) but otherwise the wizard was where Tym had left him, mid-rant.

Tym glanced at the empty flask that had contained the Whizzard potion. He stared back at the fury etched into every wrinkle on Herbit's face. Now what?

He thought hard. If he told Herbit what the potion did, the wizard would take the credit. Tym's master would sell his soul to win a WOSCAS. But the Dreamwalker had given *Tym* the knowledge, not Herbit. Tym was the Whizzard. This was his destiny. So what should he do?

The answer came like a burst of dragon-fire shooting through his brain. It was so simple! Smiling, Tym took the bottle containing the leftover Whizzard potion and hid it in a hollow tree behind the workshop. Then he picked up the flask from which he'd drunk the potion, strolled out to the well and filled the vessel with water. He ambled back, took up his position in front of Herbit, slowed down his heartbeat and…

"…Cudweed!" screamed Herbit. He blinked. He could have sworn his wretched apprentice had been over *there* a moment ago. "Stand still when I'm screeching at you! I'll give you the most severe beating your miserable flesh has ever endured!"

Tym was ready for the wizard's lunge and quickly moved sideways to avoid his clasping hands. With a loud "Arrgghhh!" Herbit went sprawling across the floor.

"Fumitory! Mullein!" The wizard picked himself up. He peered into his ransacked box and gave another ear-splitting screech. "The essences of Earth, Air and Water! Wasted! Have you any idea what I had to go through to obtain those substances?" The veins on Herbit's forehead throbbed with fury as he advanced on Tym.

"Not wasted, Master!" Tym cringed, raising his hands to defend himself. "I did it for you!"

"Eh?" The wizard scowled, but stayed his hand. "What did you say?"

"I did it for you," repeated Tym.

"Did what?"

"I had a dream, Master."

"How wonderful!" spat Herbit. "And after I've beaten you unconscious, you can have another one!"

"No, Master," said Tym quickly. "I had a wondrous vision. In it I saw you holding aloft a golden statue and hundreds of people applauding and bowing down before you."

"Oh, really. And why would they do a thing like that?"

"Because you had demonstrated a marvellous potion, Master. A potion that I had prepared by mixing the essences of Earth, Air and Water. A potion that will make you famous throughout the Dark Forest. You'll be the greatest wizard in history."

Herbit's cheek twitched. Tym had hit the right note, appealing to the Potions Master's overriding sense of vanity. The wizard eyed Tym suspiciously and considered. "What is this potion you have stumbled upon?"

Tym gulped. "With this potion," he said impressively, "you can change things into gold."

There was a silence which was only broken by the wizard's mocking laughter. "Ha! You claim to have discovered the power of transmutation! How could you, a mere toadflax, have discovered the secret of turning objects into gold? It's impossible. No Alchemist, wizard or witch in the history of the Forest has ever achieved that. No one. It can't be done."

"But in my dream…"

"Dreams! Dreams! What a dreamer you are." The wizard had taken on a malevolently playful mood. "So you can turn things into gold! This I must see."

He moved to a basket by the door and bent down, pulling out an earth-covered turnip. He threw it on to the table. "Well, Master Alchemist, turn this turnip into gold. And when you don't, I'll flay your sorry hide and make you wish you'd kept your thieving hands to yourself," he added viciously.

"Yes, Master." Tym smiled inwardly. He had told Herbit the truth and nothing but the truth. But not quite the *whole* truth. He *would* change the turnip into gold. Literally. It was Wizard Herbit who had introduced the word 'turn'. Tym would *change*, not *turn* the turnip into gold. There was a difference.

Looking determinedly at Wizard Herbit, Tym readied himself. He'd learnt from his master that magic was all in the presentation. A few 'magic' exhortations and lots of waving of arms never went amiss. He held the flask above the turnip and began to chant:

"Candle burn."

"What nonsense is this?" cried Herbit, "There are no candles burning!"

"Turnip turn."

"That's better, I suppose."

"From being old."

"Are you saying that turnip is rotten? Stick to the point."

"Into gold."

"There is no point to this mumbo-jumbo. Get on with it, bogweed!"

With a dramatic flourish of his fingers, Tym poured a single drop of 'potion' on to the turnip, bellowed "Abra…"

…and moved to Whizzard speed.

Tym picked up the turnip, walked to the door and threw the turnip into the grass, then nonchalantly wandered from Herbit's workshop back to his house, passing a crowd of statuesque villagers in various poses. At home, he reached under his bed and scrabbled at the floor, digging into the hard, packed earth before pulling out a cloth bag tied with a strong piece of twine. He opened it carefully and took out the contents. A single gold coin glistened in his hand. It was Tym's inheritance, given to him by his grandfather on his death bed.

"Here, young Tym," the old man had croaked, "I want you to have this."

"Why, Grandfather," Tym had breathed, "it's so round... and shiny... and beautiful..."

"Yes... it's my glass eye. I won't be needing it where I'm going." Then the old man had pressed a gold coin into Tym's hand. "You'd better have this as well."

The glass eye had long gone, lost in a game of marbles, but Tym still had the coin. He held it close. It was a hard decision to use the coin, but it was for a good cause and it would soon be back in its bag, safely buried in the earth.

Tym made his way back to the wizard's house, placed the coin on the table, readied himself and began to slow down.

"...cadabra!"

The wizard glanced down. His jaw dropped. He began making little gurgling noises. "G-g-g-g-gold!"

CHAPTER FOUR

How the Dreamwalker gave Tym a Dressing Down and Herbit gave him a Dressing Up.

"**W**ell, Master?" asked Tym innocently.

Wizard Herbit blinked. He picked up the shining gold coin and inspected it carefully. "It's true." The wizard's voice was husky. "Everything I went through to get those essences… my whole life, I have sought to unlock their secrets. And now, am I to be denied my prize by an untutored boy?!" He turned on Tym, his face livid with suspicion and hatred. "Steal from me, would you? Do you know the penalty for an apprentice caught…?"

"No, no, Master!" Tym shook his head hurriedly. "The potion is for you. They were your ingredients, so it is your discovery."

"Yes... yes!" The wizard's eyes shone with greed as he gazed at the coin and the flask of potion now standing beside it. "You are right. My potions... my spell... my discovery! Of course! Any discoveries made by an articled apprentice do, by highest wizardry law, belong to the master of such an aforesaid apprentice. Everyone knows that!"

Tym didn't (because Herbit had just made this 'law' up on the spot), but he breathed a sigh of relief. It looked as though he would escape a beating after all. His master was crafty enough to recognise the value of a transmutation potion.

Herbit held up the flask in one hand and Tym's inheritance in the other, and chortled. "Never have I witnessed a display of transmutation of inanimate material. No one has. Legend has it that the great Wizard Hokus Pokus once turned a prime beefsteak into a lump of charcoal, but that was at a barbecue so it probably doesn't count." He patted Tym on the shoulder and positively beamed at him. "You are right, my boy, I will be great. This will surely win me a WOSCAS! Of course, *you* may accompany me to the competition. You will be my assistant and help demonstrate the potion."

"Thank you," replied Tym with as much graciousness as he could muster. He reached out for his coin. "Shall I turn that coin back into a turnip?"

"Why on earth would you want to do that?"

Because it's mine and I want it back, thought Tym. But he couldn't say that. "To show the potion's power."

"No, no, no." The wizard fingered the coin greedily. In Herbit's opinion, avarice was a terrible thing, but poverty was worse. "Let us do the opposite. Let us turn some more objects into gold!"

Tym gulped. "Is that a good idea, Master?"

"Why shouldn't it be?"

Because I haven't got any more gold coins, thought Tym. But he said, "Because we don't want to use up all the potion before the WOSCAS."

Herbit's brow furrowed. What the boy was saying was sensible. Win a WOSCAS and you were made for life. "Hmmm. I suppose you're right," the Potions Master conceded grumpily.

With great care, he poured the 'precious' liquid from the flask into a glass phial and secured it with a cork. "Very well, we will save Herbit's Transmutation Tonic for the WOSCAS." He placed the phial in his box, secured the lid and rubbed his hands in glee. "My boy, I am going to knock 'em dead!"

That night, Tym tucked his precious bottle of Whizzard potion securely under his pillow and stretched out on his straw bed feeling ridiculously pleased with the day's events. Things couldn't have turned out any better. As he drifted off to sleep his grin was as wide as the ancient oak trees of the Forest. But if he thought he was going to have a pleasant night dreaming, Tym was sadly mistaken.

Within minutes, he found himself on the dark plain, standing before the Dreamwalker. The gargantuan figure somehow seemed darker than before.

Tym gave a nervous smile. "*Er, thank you for the recipe, it seems to be—*"

"*You corrupt your gift,*" interrupted the Dreamwalker, eyes flaring. "*You are artful, you play tricks, you deceive.*"

Tym blushed. "*I suppose I did tell Herbit a little white lie, but—*"

"*You bear false witness to the gift you have been given!*" roared the Dreamwalker, sending clouds of sand swirling across the vast emptiness.

Tym was cowed into silence.

"*Dreams should transcend the insignificant and reach beyond the worldly,*" continued the Dreamwalker.

"*Sorry,*" whispered Tym, thinking of the practical jokes he had perpetrated.

The Dreamwalker seemed to sigh. "*The gift I bestowed is for the greater good. Use it wisely. Use it with purpose and so fulfil your dreams.*"

Tym gulped. "*I will. I promise.*" It seemed the right thing to say.

"*Know this, boy,*" said the Dreamwalker solemnly. "*Those who corrupt dreams find them turning into nightmares.*"

Tym woke up sweating. His grin had vanished.

The Dreamwalker's warning seemed less worrying in daylight. However, the memory of his latest meeting with the dark colossus lay heavily on Tym's mind. Should he tell Wizard Herbit of his deception?

Tym considered the consequences of revealing his duplicity. He would be walloped to within an inch of his life. He would lose his job. He would be exposed as a fraud. Bang would go any dream he had of being a wizard.

And if he kept quiet? He'd get to go to Dun Indewood and the WOSCAS and meet other wizards. He would gain their respect and admiration. Surely this was where his destiny lay? He'd promised the Dreamwalker that he would use the gift to help fulfil his dream and he wasn't going to do that stuck in some backward village in the middle of the Forest.

Tym decided to remain silent.

As the WOSCAS drew nearer, Herbit's unbridled excitement grew. After several days of fretting about what to wear for the ceremony, he had finally ordered new robes for himself. He had even bought for Tym a star-covered tunic, purple trousers and pointy shoes, second-hand from *Elf Concern*.

"Made-to-measure," Herbit said proudly. "So you don't embarrass me in front of the great and good citizens of Dun Indewood."

Made-to-measure a dwarf, thought Tym as he squeezed into the ill-fitting garments.

There was also the matter of the acceptance speech. Herbit wanted to be fully prepared. "Just in case I win. What am I saying? Of course I'll win. No one has ever done what I'm going to do."

Or what *I'm* going to do, thought Tym.

The wizard spent hours scribbling on a scroll of parchment and forcing Tym to listen to the various drafts.

"What about this, mugwort? 'My Lords, Ladies, Gentlemen and fellow practitioners of the magical arts. Thank you. You're so right to give me this prize which I thoroughly deserve!'"

"Maybe something a little more modest, Master?"

"You think so? Hmmm. Perhaps I could weep for joy. I could hide an onion in my sleeve..." The wizard returned, muttering, to his quill and parchment.

When he wasn't doing his chores or listening to the wizard droning on, Tym worked out with a daily dose of Whizzard speed around the village, just to make sure the potion was still working. After all, he didn't know whether Whizzard speed was a permanent state or if the potion's effect would wear off. With deference to the Dreamwalker, Tym didn't indulge in any tricks on the villagers during his daily spins.

As the day of their departure for Dun Indewood dawned, Tym was at near bursting point with excitement. He hopped about as Herbit carefully packed the phial containing the 'priceless' potion into a suitably padded backpack. Tym's smaller knapsack had been packed for days, with the bottle of Whizzard potion carefully hidden away inside a roll of spare underclothes that Tym's mother referred to as his "unmentionables".

Like the majority of the inhabitants of Leafy Bottom, Tym had never ventured out of the village. Although the journey to Dun Indewood would last only a few hours (the City was little more than a league away), for Tym it was the beginning of an expedition to discover a new world. He couldn't wait to see the great metropolis.

"They say that the streets are paved with gold, Master."

"Who do?" replied Herbit.

"They do."

"And 'they' are 'who' exactly?"

"Er, I'm not sure."

"Well then. Shut up and prepare yourself."

Tym's mother had wept at his departure, crying that she would never see her baby again and making sure he'd put on clean undergarments, "just in case". Just in case what, Tym couldn't (and didn't want to) imagine.

The wizard tried to reassure her. "Madam, worry not!" he declaimed. "Your son is in good hands. And if he misbehaves, he'll feel those hands right enough!" The thought of her son in the care of a temperamental, unpredictably violent wizard seemed to have the desired calming effect on Tym's mother.

As the first rays of the rising sun filtered through the surrounding trees, and with a hundred goodbyes and good lucks from the villagers of Leafy Bottom ringing in their ears, the wizard and his apprentice set off. They headed towards the great North road that wound its way through the Forest.

"Keep to the path," warned Herbit. "You never know what's in there."

Tym peered into the depths of the Dark Forest and swore he could make out several sets of eyes, staring back at him. He decided to keep close to the wizard.

The journey to the City was uneventful. Herbit was

preoccupied with practising his speech, Tym with keeping a careful eye on the Forest and avoiding the brambles that snaked across their path. The denizens of the Forest left them alone. Herbit's reputation for mixing potions that could turn a beast into a quivering jelly in seconds went before him.

As the sun climbed to its zenith, Tym and his master saw light ahead as the trees thinned out before abruptly ending at the edge of the farmland surrounding the City.

Tym gave a gasp of wonderment. The great City of Dun Indewood! Its stone walls stood tall and pale in comparison with the darkness of the surrounding Forest. Behind the City walls, Tym could make out the towers and turrets of the Castle, sitting proudly on the hill of Bel Mont. To casual eyes, the Castle might appear to be in a state of crumbling disrepair, but to Tym it was the mightiest building he'd ever seen and a shiver of excitement ran through his body.

"Hurry along, sloeberry, or the competition will have begun before we get there."

Tym and Herbit made their way across the scrubland and approached Dun Indewood's North Gate. Groups of people milled around waiting to pass through the great oaken entrance that shut out the dangers of the Forest. Armed guards stood around, occasionally checking a wagon or stepping aside for carts driven by farmers, heading home for the small villages that lay around the walls.

The wizard pushed Tym through the gate. Together, they lined up at the guardhouse that nestled just inside the City walls. Tym glanced around at the ramshackle houses that lined the streets, which, to his disappointment, were not paved with gold. Where horses and cows had passed, they were paved with a much more organic, smellier substance.

"All right, Rolph! Your turn to check them out," a thin-faced sergeant barked into the guardhouse.

A small, round-faced guard wearing an ill fitting helmet and breastplate wandered out and eyed up the wizard and Tym. "You'll be here for the WOSCAS then?" he muttered.

The wizard was surprised. "How did you know that?"

Rolph raised an eyebrow. "On account of you wearing a silly pointy hat and long flowing robes." The Potions Master shot him a stare. Rolph seemed not to notice it, or if he did, ignored it. "There's dozens of you blokes about. The City's full. Have you got lodgin's?"

"I will stay at my usual lodgings – Mrs Scrubbemdown's B and B. There's always room at Mrs Scrubbemdown's."

"Well then, you'll be sleeping in the streets tonight – there's no rooms anywhere."

A sly look came over the wizard's face. He took Tym's gold coin from his purse and held it before Rolph's nose. "I'm sure a man with local knowledge would know where I might get a room for the night, despite the fact everywhere is full."

Rolph eyed the bribe. "A gold coin! Just for tellin' you where you can sling your hook?"

"I don't want to fish, I want lodgings."

"That's what I said." Rolph considered. "The *Fasta Pasta* restaurant might have room. Luigi the Pastafarian's just had an extension built."

"Good!" The wizard flicked the coin towards Rolph, who caught it with a flourish.

"Hey, it's not one of those magical ones is it? It's not going to disappear in a few seconds?"

Herbit gave a laugh. "No it's real. I've got plenty of those. Or I will have…" He gave Tym a knowing wink. The boy managed a sickly grin as he saw his gold coin being slipped into the guard's purse.

Then, gawping in wonder, Tym followed Herbit as the wizard strode confidently through the crowded streets. Nothing in his life in Leafy Bottom had prepared him for Dun Indewood. The City was huge, and crowded, and full of life. Every street was thronged with people and lined with traders advertising their wares:

"Swords! Daggers! Battleaxes! One-stop chopping!"

"Pies! Pies! Who's been eating all the pies?!"

"Catfood! Made from only the finest cats!"

"Designer doublets! Genuine labels! Chain mail from top chain stores!"

"Eggs! Milk! Butter! – 'ere, watch where you're goin' with that hot chestnuts barrow!" – CRASH! – "Omelettes, lovely omelettes…"

As they hurried up the winding streets that stood in the shadow of the Castle, Tym was almost deafened by the clamour from the blacksmiths' shops as the smiths hammered at strips of glowing metal, red-hot from their forges. Around a corner, he was dazzled by stalls hung about with bolts of strange materials in colours Tym would never have dreamed possible. Another turn and his nostrils were assailed by the smells from butchers' shops selling strange wobbly bits from the insides of animals. Flies rose in clouds, buzzing like a sawmill. The way twisted again and the smells of freshly baked bread from the bakers' ovens made Tym's mouth water. He closed his eyes to savour the aroma, but was woken from his reverie when Herbit gave him a sharp cuff behind the ear.

"Pay attention, cuckoo-pint! We're almost at the Castle. When we get there, behave yourself properly. Show me up, like the great goosegog that you are, and I'll flay your hide!"

Seething with resentment, Tym watched as Herbit accosted another wizard who was driving a small cart. A sign painted on the side read, **The Great Bozo, Master Of Illusion – And Dorys**. A small, fed-up looking woman was pushing the cart up the steep slope. Tym guessed she must be Dorys.

Tym had had enough. The opening rounds of the WOSCAS didn't start until later in the afternoon. Herbit would spend hours shmoozing with other wizards and giving Tym a hard time to show how masterful he was. Blow that for a lark, thought Tym. Time for some fun.

He closed his eyes in concentration. He willed his heart rate to speed up. Fast… faster… fastest…

The thousand noises of the City mingled into a soft, muted hum, throbbing at the very edge of hearing. Tym opened his eyes again and gazed around at the suddenly motionless crowd. Faster than human eyes could follow, Tym strolled away from Herbit, down a crooked path, across a rickety wooden footbridge over the foul-smelling stream of Tanner's Trickle, and out into the City.

He wandered through the silent crowds, lost in wonder at the strange sights and smells. Everywhere, people were buying and selling things, talking, arguing or just strolling about. Youths of his own age wearing identical tabards (Tym guessed they were from the Knyght School) were wandering round in groups. One was caught in the act of sprinting away with an apple he had obviously stolen from a trader's cart. The trader stood frozen, his mouth open in a yell, shaking his fist at the departing student whose friends were cheering him on.

Everywhere, the life of the City was caught out of time. Tym walked between a dog, suspended mid-bound with all four paws off the ground, and the cat it was chasing. He passed a school, where a teacher had flung a piece of chalk at a grinning student: the chalk hung in mid-air, halfway to its target. He passed workshops, where craftsmen toiled at their trade. He passed taverns full of revellers, with pipe smoke wreathed round their heads and tankards paused on the way to their lips.

At length, his wanderings led him to a district where the streets were narrower and the houses dirtier. The people looked poor. Their clothes were cheap and shoddy, and their shoulders slumped in a defeated manner. Tym wasn't sure he liked the look of this part of town, but it might prove interesting; he was getting bored with this static City. If things got nasty, he could always zip back up to Whizzard speed. He closed his eyes and slowed his body down...

...And suddenly the streets came to life. People stared at the stranger who had appeared in their midst, but only from the corners of their eyes as they scurried by, as if fearful that he might attack them.

Tym looked around with interest – and stood stock-still as he felt a hand snatch at his jerkin...

Someone was trying to rob him!

CHAPTER FIVE

How a Cutpurse left Tym a little Short in the Grumbles, and how he became Spellbound by a Lady.

With a roar of defiance, Tym spun round, his clenched right fist exploding into a terrific blow... which whistled through empty air.

"'Ere, watch it! You could have hurt me!"

The reproachful voice came from somewhere around his waist. Tym looked down... and down... into the youthful face of the smallest thief he had ever seen. He gaped at the urchin in disbelief.

"'Ow did yer know I was be'ind you, anyway?"

"Oh, let me think," said Tym sarcastically. "It might have been second sight. Or it might be a little pixie whispered it in my ear. Or it might, just possibly, have been the fact that you were practically pulling my jerkin off my back…"

"You never felt that," the small thief said decisively. "You couldn't 'ave."

"Yes, I did."

"Hands like silk I got. I could nick the fluff outta your belly button, an' you'd never know I'd got it. You never felt nuffin'!"

"Yes, I *did*."

The thief's voice took on a defensive note. "Well, you wudn't have, if you'd had pockets. I call that cheatin', goin' round wivout no purse nor no pockets neither."

Tym raised his eyebrows. "You're a pickpocket, then?"

"Pickpocket? Pickpocket?" screeched the urchin. "Who're you callin' a pickpocket? Pickpocketin's for kids. I ain't been a pickpocket since I was this high." He held a hand out level with Tym's knees. "I'm a cutpurse," he went on proudly. "Cutpurse Colyn, they call me."

"Do they? Even when you're picking pockets?"

"I *told* you, I wudn't 'ave gone to pick your pockets if you had a purse. I'd've had that away like lightnin'. I could nick the fillings out of yer teeth, you'd never know they was gone until yer found half yer choppers in yer porridge.'

Tym glanced at the sky. The sun had climbed almost to its zenith. "I'm sure. Look, I've got to get back up to the Castle…"

"I 'aven't finished robbing yer yet!" Colyn protested. "Come on, play fair. If you ain't got no purse an' you ain't got no pockets, where d'you keep yer money?"

Tym shrugged. "I haven't got any money."

Colyn was scandalised. "What, none?"

Tym shook his head apologetically.

"None at all?" Colyn looked disgusted. "How's an honest thief s'posed to make a livin' if people go round with no money, tell me that?" He gave Tym a sneer. "S'pose you ain't got no job, neither."

"Not that it's any of your business," said Tym loftily, "but I hold a junior trainee executive position in the field of experimental sorcery."

Cutpurse Colyn was unimpressed. "Oh, wizard's dogsbody, are you? Loads o' them around at the moment, up fer the WOSCAS. No use fer purse-cuttin', though. The fings some wizards keep in their purses – shouldn't be allowed." Colyn shuddered. "So yer new in town?" Tym hesitated, then nodded. "Well, you don't want to be strollin' around in The Grumbles if you don't know the score…"

"What are The Grumbles?"

Colyn waved his arms about. "Gorblimey, don't you know nuffin'? *This* is The Grumbles. Dodgiest part of town, specially for a straw-chewin' country bumpkin like you…"

"Oy! Watch it!"

Colyn sighed heavily. "Typical," he moaned. "What a day. First purse I cut, Old Granny Spoon, nothin' in it but a couple o' mint humbugs. Then I dun Gilbut the Graverobber. I won't tell you what he 'ad in his purse, it'd turn yer stomack. And now, you. Ah well…" Colyn gave a sigh and reached inside the depths of his jerkin, producing a silver coin. "I'm just too kind for my own good. Here y'are," he went on, holding out the money to Tym. "Just don't tell me old dad. He'd have kittens if he knew I was giving away the profits." He thrust the coin into Tym's hand.

Tym was at a loss. "Er, thank you…" He opened his hand. The coin had gone!

Colyn held it up. He had a huge grin on his face. "Told you I was good!" he said smugly, pocketing the coin. "Anyway, if yer 'ere fer the WOSCAS yer'd better get yer skates on. They'll be startin' any minute."

"I suppose you're right." Tym looked around helplessly. "Erm… which way…?"

"Oh, blimey! Do I have to do everyfing for yer?" Colyn rolled his eyes. "Down there, first left, second right, over the bridge and up the hill. The Castle's a big buildin' with battlements," he went on as Tym closed his eyes. "Yer can't miss it—"

Colyn broke off suddenly and blinked. The stranger had completely disappeared. Colyn rubbed his eyes. "Where'd 'e go?" He stood for a while in thought. Then he appeared to come to a decision. With firm (if short) steps, Cutpurse Colyn struck out across the narrow street and set off up the hill, towards the Castle.

"Where in the Forest have you been?"

Tym watched the wizard's twitching hands and decided on a diplomatic approach. "Sorry, Master. I suppose I must have got separated from you in the crowds."

"I'll deal with you later!" Herbit was not mollified. "Stand behind me and don't draw attention to yourself!"

The Great Hall of the Castle of Dun Indewood had been specially decorated for the occasion. Brightly coloured draperies festooned the stone walls. Wizards of all shapes and sizes milled around. Some wore formal robes and gazed about them with an air of condescension. Others, obviously their country cousins from the outlying villages of the Dark Forest, stared at all this finery with expressions that ranged from curiosity to bafflement.

An elderly wizard in a plain brown robe sat in a high chair from which he could view the proceedings. Tym tugged Herbit's sleeve. "Master, who is he?"

Herbit gave him an exasperated glance. "If it's any of your business, bogbean, that is the Runemaster – the Chief Wizard of Dun Indewood." The Potions Master's face took on a mean, discontented look. "Look at him, Lord Muck now, isn't he? I remember when he was nothing but a penniless hedge-wizard, without a farthing to bless himself."

A small figure stepped up to the Runemaster's chair and whispered in his ear. "Who's he?" asked Tym.

"What do you think I am, a guide book?" the Potions Master hissed savagely. "If you must know, that's Humfrey the Boggart. He works with the Runemaster. *Boggart and Rune* they call themselves: Private Inquestigators – they claim they can solve mysteries before they happen. Well, of course, anybody can be clairvoyant if they have second sight. I don't see what's so special about…"

But Tym had stopped listening. For that matter, he'd stopped breathing. He was staring at a tall, dark-haired girl who had stepped through the curtains behind the Runemaster and now sat in the seat next to him with a look of aristocratic hauteur on her face.

When he remembered to take another breath, Tym asked, "Who's *she*?"

Herbit gave Tym a knowing look. "She is the Lady Zamarind, granddaughter and sole heir of Robat, High Lord of Dun Indewood. She's our Patron. She'll be handing out the WOSCAS to the winners." Herbit grinned nastily. "Forget it, my fine forest buck. You haven't got a chance!"

Tym continued to gaze open mouthed at Zamarind. Her hair... and her eyes... her hands... her nose... her mouth...

The Runemaster whispered to Zamarind, who gave a little frown of annoyance and clapped her hands. The opening demonstrations of the WOSCAS began. Tym was too entranced by the Lady Zamarind to follow these examples of wizardly skill very closely, but he was dimly aware that most of the contestants weren't very good.

There was Albut the Treekeeper, who planted an acorn in a pot, poured water over it and chanted a mystical incantation that he said would guarantee that the acorn would grow into a great oak tree before their very eyes. Questioned by the Runemaster, Albut had to admit that this miracle would take about a hundred years to complete and retired in a fit of the sulks.

Rather more impressive, though slightly sickening, was Abanaza the Magnificent, who reached into a rabbit and pulled out a top hat. The Great Bozo mystified the crowd with the famous illusion of sawing a lady in half. (He was later spotted painting out the '**And Dorys**' bit from the sign on his cart.)

After a few dozen more substandard feats of magic, Herbit's name was called: he strode forward confidently. "Fellow wizards," he declaimed, "and Citizens of Dun Indewood; my Lords, Ladies and Gentlemen! Today I shall demonstrate, for your delight and edification, a potion of my own devising with the power to change everyday objects to gold! I call it, Herbit's Transmutation Tonic!"

There was a moment of silence, then a few muffled sniggers from the crowd. The Lady Zamarind looked interested for the first time. The Runemaster leaned forward and fixed Herbit with a hard stare. "Dost thou truly claim to have solved the mystery that hath defeated the greatest minds of wizardry throughout all history?"

Herbit quailed, but his nerve held. "Aye, my Lord."

The Runemaster leaned back, sighing gustily. "Oh, well, so long as we know."

Tym heard Humfrey the Boggart mutter something that sounded like, "Thish, I musht shee."

Herbit reached into his pack and took out the phial of potion... then spun round in astonishment as Tym stepped forward.

"Observe," cried Tym in a loud voice, never taking his eyes off the Lady Zamarind. He held his hands, palms out, towards the audience. "Nothing in my hands!" He rolled up the arms of his threadbare jerkin. "Nothing up my sleeves!"

"And nothing between your ears!" hissed Herbit, scowling

furiously at his assistant. "Stop making an exhibition of yourself before I flay you alive!"

Tym stepped back. He reached into Herbit's pack and and took out a carrot which he placed on a pedestal in front of the dais on which the Runemaster and Zamarind sat. At least he'd made the Lady Zamarind look at him, though he couldn't tell whether she was impressed or not. Tym stood aside, closed his eyes and concentrated as Herbit let a drop of 'Transmutation Tonic' fall on to the carrot…

…And as the crowd fell still, Tym stepped forward, picked up the carrot and strolled out of the Great Hall, out of the Castle, down the winding streets to the market where he slipped under the arm of a fat merchant, opened his purse, took out a gold coin (if Cutpurse Colyn could move as fast as I can, he thought, he'd be the best in the business), replaced it with the carrot (after all, he reassured himself, fair exchange is no robbery), set off back up the hill – a bit slower this time – back into the Castle, up the steps to the Great Hall, put the gold coin down where the carrot had been, stepped back and closed his eyes…

A gasp went around the hall. Herbit the Potions Master raised his arms with a look of triumph as applause burst out.

The Lady Zamarind leaned forward. Her eyes sparkled.

The Runemaster sat bolt upright. His eyes widened.

Humfrey the Boggart leaned against a pillar. His eyes narrowed.

And among the crowds at the back of the hall, a pair of eyes closer to the ground than all the others glinted. A hushed voice whispered to itself, "Well now – there's a fing!"

CHAPTER SIX

O f Wine, Wizards and Old Sea Dogs, and
Pizza among Thieves.

"Another wagon of fline, Landlord!" Herbit's slurred
bellow echoed round the restaurant. Luigi the Pastafarian
wiggled his eyebrows at Tym and bustled out to fill a stone
flagon from the barrel in the cellar. The Potions Master was
celebrating his success with free drinks all round.

His 'transformation spell' had caused a sensation.
Humfrey the Boggart had taken the coin and bitten it.
Then he'd whispered something to the Runemaster, who'd
given Herbit a hard stare and stroked his beard
thoughtfully. He'd looked to Tym as if he would have loved
an excuse to disqualify the Potions Master for cheating, if

only he could work out how he'd done it.

But as far as anyone could tell, Herbit really had produced a gold coin from a carrot. Every test his incredulous fellow wizards had been able to devise had simply confirmed the fact. Herbit was through to the final of the WOSCAS. Bertole the Weather Monger was beside himself with jealousy, which made Herbit's triumph even sweeter.

Following his triumph, Herbit had spent his newly 'transformed' gold coin on a room at Luigi the Pastafarian's *Pizza Palace and Premier Comfort Lodge Hotel* (formerly known as *Fasta Pasta on the Piazza*). In answer to Herbit's enquiry, Luigi had nodded until the beads on his multicoloured dreadlocks rattled. "You got'a lucky! The builders only jus' finished the extensive development o' luxury eggzekertive one sweet studio apartments."

Herbit's eyes narrowed. "One sweet?"

"Sure. Ev'ry night, before you go to bed, I leave one sweet on you' pillow. In a crinkly wrapper!" Luigi hastened to reassure him.

"Studio apartments?"

"Hokay, you get a mattress onna floor. You can call it a sofa an' lie on it an' make it into a bed, or you can call it a bed an' sit on it an' make it into a sofa. What'a you expect for five groats a week?"

So now Herbit was sitting amid a crowd of sozzled well-wishers who had no interest in the WOSCAS, and didn't really know who the wizard was, and didn't care as long as he kept buying them wine. Loudest of the group was a ruffianly figure in a threadbare frock coat and a three-cornered hat. He had a hook on the end of his leg, with which he lashed viciously at anyone who looked like helping themselves to his drink, and a peg-arm, which he beat upon the table as he sang roistering songs of the sea:

"Oh, I'm a proud sailor, both hearty and true,
For I've tacked round the Horn in a leaky canoe:
I rounded the Cape in a South-western gale
With naught in my guts but a gallon of ale...

Which came right up again with a yo-heave-ho, maties ..."

This was Captain Gorge, Luigi had explained to Tym. The captain was one of Luigi's regulars. His face was mostly a big, warty nose, which poked out between a thicket of beard and a villainous-looking eyepatch. His one good eye was small and red and glinted with unholy mischief.

"Avast there, me hearties!" roared the captain, waving his cup about so that most of his wine sploshed over the people sitting near him. "Slubber me backstays with cod liver oil! Scupper me scantlin's and heave on me hawsehole, let's have three hearty hurrahs for the fine bucko who's standin' us all grog, with a yo-heave-ho and a bucket of blood!"

Herbit stood up unsteadily to acknowledge the addled cheers and bowed to the captain. "Am I to take it that you are a sailor, sir?" he asked carefully.

Captain Gorge slammed his peg-arm down on the table. "Aye, sir! Man and buntline, forty years before the mizzen. Skin pickled in the brine o' the boundin' billows, heart of oak and burgoo in me blood!" Herbit bowed again and nearly fell over. The captain started to sing once more.

"What shall we do with the sunken dribbler?
What shall we do with the sunken dribbler?
What shall we do with the sunken dribbler?
Halyard in the marline..."

Tym sidled over to the bar, where the Pastafarian was wiping glasses and smiling the happy smile of a restaurant owner watching his profits soar as the wine levels in the drinkers' cups went down. Tym tugged Luigi's sleeve. "Is Captain Gorge really a sailor?" he asked.

Tym had never seen the sea. Nobody in Dun Indewood or its surrounding villages had. It was a legend. Some of the old stories and songs told of a vast expanse of water, so big that you couldn't see to the other side. Tym couldn't imagine this. There were only a few streams and pools in the Dark Forest, mostly haunted by water sprites. The biggest (and only) river he'd seen was Tanner's Trickle, the foul stream that oozed its way through Dun Indewood on a bed which mostly consisted of the bones of cormorants that had unwisely tried to fish in its rancid waters.

Luigi shrugged. "I mean," Tym persisted, "the sea's miles and miles away, if it even exists at all. And ships don't sail up the Trickle, do they? It's not deep enough."

Luigi turned to face him. "My fren', I don' know. Long time ago, the Trickle was a big river. My ancestors come from over the sea in a ship an' start the first pasta restaurant in Dun

Indewood." Luigi spread his arms wide with a look of proprietorial pride. "Us Pastafarians, we's still here. But the sea? Gone."

"Aye, maties!" Luigi was interrupted by the Captain's roar. "There I was, lashed to the stump o' the the mast wi' forty fathom o' whipping yarn, a bottle of grog in one hand, a belayin' pin in the other an' the ship's wheel between my teeth…"

Tym listened, enthralled, as Captain Gorge's tale rambled to its incoherent conclusion. He didn't understand a quarter of what the captain said, but his talk of strange seas and foreign shores sounded exciting and adventurous. The captain certainly had plenty of eager listeners: in fact, he was beginning to attract attention away from Herbit. The wizard clearly resented the fact that the old sailor was stealing his thunder, especially as Herbit was paying for the drinks. (Captain Gorge, Tym noticed, hadn't bought a round all night.)

At length, Herbit weaved his way to the captain's table, and prodded him in the chest with a wavering finger. "Where's y'ship?" he demanded truculently. "If y'r a cap'n, where's y'ship? Ha?"

The captain didn't bellow as Tym expected. A cunning glint crept into his eye. "Never mind that, me bucko." The old sailor's dreadful beard jutted at a menacing angle. "If you're a wizard, show us a trick."

Herbit straightened his shoulders. "Ver' well," he said with unsteady dignity. He clicked his fingers successfully at the third attempt. Luigi waddled over. "Lan'lord," Herbit said with dignity, "bring me an aubergi… an auber… a tomato."

Tym watched with resignation as Luigi placed a tomato on

the table in front of the Potions Master. Herbit took the phial of liquid from his robes and, with an unsteady hand, poured out a few drops…

…The cheers and catcalls of the revellers died away as Tym went to Whizzard speed, took the tomato and left the restaurant. He scrambled through the window of Bottomly Scraggs, the moneylender next door, exchanged the tomato for a gold crown piece, returned to Luigi's and placed the coin on the table…

There were "ooohs" of wonder from the watchers. Several hands reached for the coin, but Gorge's peg-arm slammed down with the speed of a striking snake, squishing several unwary fingers in the process.

The captain eyed the coin closely, then let out a huge bellow of laughter. The wicks on the candles guttered in the blast and the wine bottles that held them danced in their raffia baskets.

"Luff me snotter and leech me with a gudgeon pin," roared the old sailor. "I take it all back, me hearty. 'Tis a fine, powerful wizard y'are and no mistake!" There was an outburst of cheering and many hands were raised to slap the gratified Potions Master on the back.

Perhaps only Tym noticed Captain Gorge get up, collect a pile of flat, greasy boxes from Luigi and slip silently through the door of the restaurant, out into the night.

To the casual onlooker, the clearing appeared to be no different from any other in the Dark Forest. Unfortunately, the casual onlooker who chanced upon this spot would suddenly find himself blindfolded and bundled away, stripped of everything valuable by rough and unsympathetic hands, and left to hang upside down from a tree while he pondered the folly of being casual about anything in the Dark Forest. For this clearing was the Forest home of the King of Thieves.

The Thieves of the Dark Forest weren't simply a collection of pilferers and thugs: they were professionals and good at their job. They had to be. The Dark Forest was not a forgiving place for the unwary. The thieves came and went from Dun Indewood at will. They robbed travellers on the Forest roads, when there were any travellers to rob. Otherwise, they would steal from the City and lie low in the Forest until the hue and cry had died down.

The King of Thieves was, by definition, the best of the thieves. He was brave, resourceful and daring. If he had a weakness, it was that he found being a parent a lot harder than being a cut-throat.

"I told you, dad!" said Colyn in tones of profound exasperation, "I *told* you, this ol' geezer I seen, 'e can change fings into gold. Carrots an' stuff."

The King of Thieves rubbed his eyes wearily. "Look, my son. Carrots is not gold. Turnips is not gold. Root vegetables of any kind is not gold. Gold is gold. It don't grow from seeds. Miners mine it, goldsmiths work it, rich folks spend it, merchants make it, we nick it."

"Well, 'e did," muttered Colyn sulkily.

His father was saved from replying by a bellow that echoed around the clearing. "Ahoy, me hearties!"

Instantly, the glade was full of running figures. All clustered round the swaggering figure of Captain Gorge, eager hands snatching at pizza boxes.

The King of Thieves glared at Gorge. Trying to talk sense to his son always made him irritable. "Well, it's about time!" he complained. "Where have you been all this while and what have you been doing?"

"Belay and avast, shiver me timbers and splice me leechlines, matey—" Captain Gorge broke off as the King of Thieves grabbed his jerkin in a grip of iron.

"That's enough o'that, lardbelly. Save the jolly jack tar stuff for them as is impressed by it. I don't believe you've ever been on a ship. All that grog's addled yer brains – it never 'appened, none of it." Several thieves sniggered. "We sent you out for pizzas hours ago, 'cos we wuz all fed up with eatin' acorns an' wild deer – an' what do you do? Sit on your fat backside drinkin' like a bucket while we all wait 'ere with our belly buttons shakin' 'ands with our backbones."

Gorge drew himself up with dignity. "Shackle me futtocks, Admiral, it takes time to make four-and-twenty pizzas. What's more, I made good use of me time, reeve me jackyards if I didn't—"

"'Ere!" complained a thief, holding up a soggy slice of pizza. "This has got anchovies on it!"

"I seen a very interestin' phernomernon, I did, me hearty. I seen—"

70

"I hate anchovies."

Captain Gorge tried again. "I seen—"

"They give me gripes in me gizzard."

"I seen—"

"You start me on anchovies and on your own head be it."

Gorge gave a roar of rage. "Never mind your blasted anchovies! I'm tryin' to tell the Admiral 'ere what I seen! I seen—"

"Olives," cut in another thief in mournful tones. "Can't stand olives!"

"I seen this wizard!" screamed Gorge at the top of his voice. "I seen 'im change a tomato into a gold coin! There now!"

"See!" Colyn's voice was shrill with triumph. "See, dad? I *told* you!"

The King of Thieves regarded his spy with scorn. "You've been had!" he said. "Wizards've been tryin' that for years. They can't do it. It was just a conjurin' trick. The sorta fing that wouldn't fool a baby: only a great lummox like you!"

Gorge bristled with anger. "I seen what I seen, blast me with barnacles and poop me athwartships! He poured a few drops of potion on the tomato an' it turned into a crown piece, as I live an' breathe."

The King of Thieves continued to look scornful, but a calculating glint had crept into his eyes.

"He's right, Dad!" Colyn piped up. "And 'e's got this assistant wot can make himself invisible. I met 'im."

"A wizard that can turn fings into gold," mused the King

of Thieves. "And an assistant who can go anywhere without being seen. I'd like to meet these interestin' people." He gave a villainous grin and rubbed his hands together. "If you're right, I fink our careers are about to take off in a whole new direction!"

CHAPTER SEVEN

How Tym turned a Guard into Gold, and Humfrey turned Victory into Defeat.

The courtyard of the Castle of Dun Indewood was crowded to overflowing. The WOSCAS awards ceremony was a glittering occasion. All the poor people who couldn't afford seats in the Great Hall were crammed into the courtyard outside to see the City's notables arrive. Lords, Knyghts and their Ladies arrived in sleek carriages and waved at the cheering crowds. Various contestants were being sketched by engravers and interviewed by town criers who would later announce the results to the rest of the City and its surrounding villages.

Herbit was talking to the town crier from Leafy Bottom.

"Well, Garf, of course, it's the ultimate honour to be nominated for an award by one's fellow wizards. Whoever wins, it's just such a thrill being here…"

The contestants waved to the hordes of fans and passed through the great doors into the Hall itself, under the glare of several witches who were huddled in a discontented group muttering that their magic was as good as wizard magic any day, trust men to make a lot of fuss about themselves and leave the womenfolk out, not that they'd want to show themselves up by doing tricks in front of people like a pack of performing dogs…

Tym, carrying Herbit's bag as well as his own knapsack, had mixed feelings about the WOSCAS. After all, it was *his* magic that everybody was getting excited about, but Herbit was taking all the credit: and, if he won, the Potions Master would be more insufferable than ever. On the plus side, Tym would also automatically get a WOSCAS as 'Best Supporting Wizard', so some of the glory would rub off on him. Then the Lady Zamarind might notice him…

Inside, the Great Hall was packed to the rafters. The draperies were lit by brightly coloured lanterns; above these, sparkling stars shone in the darkness beneath the ceiling, and planets revolved round each other in a slow and complicated dance while comets and meteorites with burning tails shot here, there and everywhere.

As before, the Runemaster sat in his high chair: on this occasion, he was dressed in the regalia of the Grand Mage of the Magic Rectangle. Humfrey the Boggart stood by the Runemaster's side looking watchful and suspicious. The

Lady Zamarind had not yet appeared.

All round the Hall, people were being nice to other people they couldn't stand. There were lots of forced grins and strained laughter. To one side of the Runemaster's dais, a selection of popular tunes (at least, Tym assumed they must be popular with *somebody*) was being played by Woody Holly and the Chestnuts. Tym found the seats reserved for himself and Herbit (who was twitching with nerves) and waited for the competition to begin.

There were three categories to be decided, with three finalists in each: Best Illusionist, Best Conjurer and – Herbit's category – Best Spellbinder. All the contestants in each category would perform feats of magic and then a panel of senior wizards would judge the winner.

The conversation stilled and thunderous applause broke out as the Lady Zamarind appeared. She waved regally to the cheering crowd and took her seat. The roar of the crowd became the soft trilling of songbirds in Tym's ears. He gazed at Zamarind with spaniel eyes and sighed like a bellows. Herbit gave his assitant one disgusted glance and then retired into a fretful private world of apprehension, biting his nails and checking his cloak for the umpteenth time to see that the potion was still there.

Zamarind clapped her hands and the Grand Final of the WOSCAS began.

LeRoy the Magnificent produced an illusion of a great dragon which hovered over the crowd, shooting from its mouth a multitude of fireworks which exploded with banshee shrieks and multicoloured streaks of flame. Greggery the

Tasteless turned the Great Hall into an enchanted forest dell where a shimmering waterfall fell into a gurgling stream, deer and squirrels frolicked and butterflies flitted from flower to flower. Everyone went "Aaah". Zakkary the Unpleasant created an illusion that the Great Hall was a haunted castle: ghosts, efreets and spectres soared screeching and gibbering overhead, while zombies, ghouls and skeletons lurched through the terrified crowd.

The Runemaster stood and waved a hand. The horrible illusions vanished. The crowd settled down. The judges conferred. At length, the senior judge wrote something on a card, sealed it in a golden envelope and handed it to Humfrey who, in turn, passed it to the Lady Zamarind.

She stood and held up the envelope. There was an expectant hush. In ringing tones, she announced: "And the winner is..." she tore open the envelope "...LeRoy the Magnificent!"

"Knew he'd get it," said a small wizard on Tym's right over the roar of applause. "They never give awards for Horror."

The successful wizard made a great show of being astounded and overwhelmed. He stumbled from his seat, humbly accepting the insincere congratulations of his fellow wizards, and took the small golden statuette of a wizard in flowing robes and a pointy hat from Zamarind.

He turned to the crowd, his eyes brimming with tears: "My dear, dear friends... this isn't for me... it's for all the little people..." At which point he broke down and had to be led away by his dear, dear friends, all of whom (as he knew very well) were heartily wishing him dead.

The Conjuring WOSCAS was won by Walta the Prestidigitator, who produced a four-course banquet for all the guests (including coffee, liqueurs and after-dinner mints) and was hailed winner by popular acclaim.

Then it was the turn of the Spellbinders. Gerimee the Miraculous made the mistake of offering a charm to turn a beautiful young woman into a hideous old crone, but couldn't find anyone willing to be subjected to it. Getting flustered, he then offered a charm to turn a hideous old crone into a beautiful young woman, but since none of the ladies present would admit to being hideous old crones, this didn't work either and Gerimee was disqualified.

Kornelius the Enchanter's Explosive Enlarger was certainly impressive. In many ways it was a shame that he chose to demonstrate it on a small carniverous spider which, on becoming a giant carniverous spider, promptly ate Kornelius, putting him right out of the running.

When the spider had been shrunk to normal size, and the panic its appearance had caused had abated, Herbit the Potions Master stepped forward. All his nerves had disappeared. He knew that he had only to produce a minor miracle and the coveted WOSCAS was as good as his.

"My Lords, Knyghts, fellow Wizards, Ladies and Gentlemen," he announced, "I shall now demonstrate the wonder of this or any other age: Herbit's Transmutation Tonic!"

There was eager applause: news of Herbit's success in the qualifying round had spread. If there was one thing the people of Dun Indewood liked, it was gold in large quantities.

Herbit gestured to Tym, who produced a parsnip from under his jerkin and held it up.

"Shay, Mishter Wizard!"

Herbit paused. Humfrey the Boggart detached himself from the pillar against which he had been leaning for most of the proceedings, and now sauntered forward. He stood staring at Herbit and rubbing his chin. "That Transhmutation Tonic of yoursh – does it work on anything?"

Herbit drew himself up proudly. "Anything, sir!"

"That'sh shome claim. OK." Humfrey jerked his thumb. "Try shome on thish guard here."

"Certainly," boomed Herbit with sublime confidence.

Tym's stomach churned as the hulking guard stepped forward with a bashful grin and a wave to his fellow guards, who stood nudging each other and making ribald comments. Humfrey must be suspicious! Why else would he 'volunteer' the guard for Herbit's demonstration? And why had Herbit agreed?

It was too late to protest. Herbit, standing on a stool, was already dribbling a drop of potion on to the grinning guard's helmet. Tym willed his heart to speed up…

…And the Great Hall and everyone in it dropped out of Tym's timeframe. All movement ceased. Even the flies battering themselves against the high windows stopped in mid-buzz.

Tym's mind raced. The guard was obviously too heavy for him to lift. An idea struck him. He raced out of the Hall and through the courtyard to where a section of Castle wall was being repaired by a gang of workmen. A wheelbarrow full of stones stood to one side of the motionless group – one of whom, Tym noticed, was about to be hit on the head by a falling hammer dropped by a careless workmate high above. Tym tipped the stones out of the barrow and wheeled it away.

And paused. No, it was none of his business. He went on.

And paused. The Dreamwalker had accused Tym of corrupting his gift. Of not using it for good. Was he about to prove the strange creature right?

Tym went back. He stood on tiptoe and pushed the falling hammer two feet to the left, where it would drop harmlessly just behind the workman it had been about to hit.

Then he picked up the wheelbarrow again and trundled it back into the Great Hall.

Tym folded up the unmoving guard and, with great effort, dumped him in the wheelbarrow. With every muscle creaking, he pushed it back out of the Hall, across the courtyard and out of the Castle. Perspiring and groaning with the effort, he rolled his burden along the cobbled streets, weaving through the still and silent crowds, until he reached a deserted stable he had noticed the day before.

Tym lugged the unresisting guard into the stable and laid him down on a pile of rotting straw. He searched until he found a length of rope, which he used to tie the guard up as tightly as he could. He 'borrowed' a piece of rag from a linen-maker's workshop a few doors down the street and stuffed it into the man's mouth.

Then he left the guard and raced across town to the banking district. He had to hope the man wouldn't be found until he and Herbit had collected their WOSCAS and were well away from Dun Indewood. As to what would happen after that, Tym had no idea. Maybe he'd run away into the Forest – maybe he'd jump into a bottomless chasm. But first things first.

He sneaked past unseeing guards into the strongroom at Barkleaf's Bank and picked up a gold ingot from a pile. After all, Tym reasoned, if a carrot turns into a gold coin, a human being would have to turn into something bigger. He wasn't really stealing the gold… he was a victim of circumstance… he'd put it back later…

Back at the castle, Tym set the ingot on the pedestal where the guard had stood. He stepped back and forced his heart rate to slow. The scene around him flowed back into life…

…As the audience of the WOSCAS caught its collective breath. The guard had gone! In his place was a gold ingot! There was a moment of stunned silence, followed by a perfect tidal wave of applause. Herbit stood beaming, arms aloft, accepting the accolades. There was cheering and stamping and whistling. Without waiting for an envelope, the Lady Zamarind leapt to her feet and cried, "And the winner is…"

"Hold everything!" Humfrey's barked command cut through the din like a whiplash. The applause died away uncertainly as the boggart looked Wizard Herbit straight in the eye.

"Very impresshive," drawled Humfrey. "OK, hot shtuff.

Now try that trick on me…" A murmur ran round the Hall as the boggart paused, then went on: "…with all the doorsh locked from the outshide."

At a signal from the boggart, guards around the Hall stepped out through the doors and closed them behind them. There was a rattle of turning keys. Confidently, Herbit dribbled a drop of potion on to Humfrey's head…

…Tym, at Whizzard speed, raced from door to door, rattling at the handles, pounding at the unyielding wood. It was no good. Humfrey had planned his trap well. The doors were impassable, the windows were too high, there was nothing with which Tym could fashion a ladder. Numb with misery and dread, he allowed his heart rate to slow…

…Herbit blinked. He dripped a few more drops from his phial on to Humfrey's head. Humfrey gave him a nasty grin. In a panic, Herbit tipped the enitre contents of his phial over the boggart. Herbit's potion dribbled round his ears and Humfrey's grin got wider.

Herbit stammered, "It d-d-doesn't work…"

The boggart turned to the Runemaster. "What'd I shay? Didn't I tell ya? The guy'sh a fraud – a fake – a phoney."

"But… but… but…" Herbit looked dazed.

The Runemaster rose. "Wretch!" he thundered. "False wizard! Thou has sought to decieve thy brethren!"

"No, my Lord." Tym's voice was quiet, but it dropped into the stillness following the Runemaster's denunciation like a stone into a pond. He stepped forward.

The Runemaster stared hard at Tym. "What meanest thou, lad?"

Tym felt every eye on him. He had everyone's full attention, even the Lady Zamarind's. His face burned with shame: but there was no help for it. The game was up. "I am Wizard Herbit's apprentice, my Lord," he said quietly. "My master did not knowingly deceive you. I deceived him."

The Runemaster eyed him narrowly. "How so? Who art thou to deceive a Master of Magical Lore? Art thou a wizard?"

"No, my Lord," said Tym miserably. "I am a *Whizzard*." Haltingly, Tym explained. Ripples of comment spread out around him as the crowd digested the news. Herbit's face grew more thunderous at each revelation. At the end of his confession, Tym stood with head bowed.

"Let me shee if I got this shtraight," said Humfrey. "When Herbit did his sho-called Transhmutationsh, what really happened wash that you shwiped whatever it wash he wash transhmutating, and fetched gold to put in itsh place."

Tym nodded dumbly. Humfrey nodded appreciatively. "Runie and I knew the whole thing musht be a shcam: turning a carrot into gold, OK, but into a gold *coin*?" Humfrey shook his head. "But we couldn't work out how it wash done. Neat trick. Where'sh the guard you vanished?"

Tym told him. At a signal from the Runemaster, four guards set off to collect (and, no doubt, have fun at the expense of) their luckless colleague.

Herbit rounded on Tym. "Crowsfoot! Devil's bit!" The Potions Master was wild-eyed and quivering with indignation. "You have humiliated me... ruined me... dashed all my hopes!" Herbit looked Tym straight in the eye. "How did you do it? How did you discover the secret of the essences when I, with all my knowledge, tried for years and failed?"

Tym told him. Herbit was silent for a moment. When he spoke again, his voice was broken. "Blood. Three drops of my blood would have unlocked the power I have sought all my life and I never knew it." Herbit caught his breath in a sob. Then he lifted his head and his voice strengthened. "Know this, false apprentice. The essences that you stole are precious and dangerous. They are not come by easily. I won them with much pain, and you will know much pain in using them." The Potions Master shook his fist at Tym. "My curse upon you, boy! You have made me a laughing stock—"

"Nay!" The Runemaster's voice was harsh. "Thou didst that thyself when thou sought to claim thy apprentice's discovery as thy own." The Runemaster stood and pointed an accusing finger. "Thou art hereby disqualified from this competition – and expelled from the Company of the Magic Rectangle."

There was a rumble of agreement and an outbreak of boos and hissing from the audience. With a final, furious glance at Tym, Herbit the Potions Master gathered what shreds of dignity remained to him and stalked out of the Hall.

The Runemaster remained standing. "Be it known," he announced in a voice that carried to every corner of the Hall, "that the Award for Best Spellbinder is awarded – posthumously – to Kornelius the Enchanter." He turned to Tym, his face grave. "As for thee… thou hast cast thine own doom. The penalty for the false practice of magic is laid down from the earliest times, and there can be no excuse and no appeal." The old man turned to the Lady Zamarind. "My Lady, thou knowest what must be done."

Zamarind hesitated. She turned to the Runemaster and said, "My Lord, must it be so? He is young and meant no harm…"

The Runemaster shook his head heavily. 'The Lore is the Lore."

Zamarind bit her lip and nodded. Then she stood and held up one hand for silence. "Then, so must it be. Tym, wizard's apprentice, you are to leave the City and Dominions of Dun Indewood by the shortest way, never to return. You are banished into the Dark Forest. For ever!"

CHAPTER EIGHT

How Tym fell among Thieves and stood in
Peril of his Weasand.

Carrying only his knapsack, Tym left the Castle with
dragging steps. He was closely watched by four nervous and
unfriendly guards, who didn't appreciate Tym's treatment of
their hapless colleague and certainly didn't intend to allow
anything of the sort to be practised on them. They needn't
have worried. Tym was hardly aware of their presence, or of
anything else apart from his own misery. He'd barely even
thought of escape. Even if he went into Whizzard speed,
where could he run to? He'd have to slow down to normal
speed sooner or later and he had nowhere in the City
to hide.

"Serves you right," the guard sergeant told Tym vindictively. "Leavin' poor old Smudger tied up like that, with his weakness and all. Banished to the Forest! Know what that means, don't you?" Without waiting for Tym to reply the sergeant went on in a gloating voice, "It means you'll never be allowed to come back here to the City, nor none of the villages hereabouts, not if you were to live for a hundred years!"

"Mind you, Sarge," said another guard, "in the Forest, he won't live for a hundred years."

"He'll be lucky if he lasts five minutes," chipped in a third. The guards guffawed.

Tym choked back a sob. He knew very well what banishment meant. He could never go home to his mother. He would never learn how to be a wizard. He would never see the Lady Zamarind again. His glazed eyes didn't register the scene beside the Castle walls, where a stonemason was furiously scolding a sheepish-looking labourer; another worker, in a daze, was staring at a hammer lying at his feet and muttering over and over again, "Two feet to the right and that would've killed me... two feet, that's all..."

He was unaware of the gathering dusk and the curious crowds that stopped what they were doing to watch him being escorted by. He didn't hear the sympathetic murmur of "Good luck, lad," from Rolph the Gatekeeper. The only sound that woke him from his brooding despondency was the crash of the City's great wooden gates as they slammed behind him for the last time.

At the sound, Tym paused – but forced himself not to look

back. He had been banished from the whole world that he knew. His only home now was the unknown and terrible wilderness of the Dark Forest.

The last of the daylight drained from the sky as Tym reached the eaves of the endless trees, and the shadows beneath them seemed to reach out to draw him into their gloomy embrace. A pale half-moon rose. In the dim light that slanted down through the trees, a shadow detached itself from a pool of inky darkness and stepped forward into Tym's path.

"Well, helllooooo!"

Tym looked up glumly and took in the figure standing before him. It was wearing a frock coat (over rather frayed linen) and knee britches, despite the fact that it was obviously not human. In a flat, dead voice, Tym said, "You're a wolf, aren't you?"

The creature drew itself up proudly. "I am a *Highway*wolf."

"Right, whatever. I suppose you're going to eat me now."

The wolf was nonplussed for a moment. This was a departure from the usual script, which at this point generally went along the lines of, "No, no, spare me, please, I'll do anything, mercy, mercy, I beg of you, aaaaaarrrggghhhh!"

"Well, er... yes."

"Good. Where would you like to start?"

"Well, I would usually leap into a savage and frenzied attack on your defenceless throat..."

"Fine, fine. Would you like me to take my neckerchief off?"

To its own surprise, the wolf's voice became shrill. "Now, look here, this simply isn't fair. You're not playing the game.

You're just trying to put me off my stroke – well it won't work, so there." The wolf bared its fangs in a truly terrifying snarl. "Ready or not, here I come!" It gathered itself to leap.

"'Ello, Wolfie."

The wolf sagged. "Oh, for pity's sake," it muttered.

The King of Thieves sauntered out from a thicket and gave the wolf a big, friendly grin. The wolf glared at the outlaw. "You're not alone, I suppose?"

"Don't be silly." The King of Thieves snapped his fingers. Bushes rustled all along each side of the path.

"No, too much to hope for," muttered the wolf disgustedly. A plaintive note crept into its voice as it waved a paw at Tym. "When you've finished with him, can I have the bones?" There was a sound of arrows being notched to bowstrings and swords being loosened in their sheaths. "Only asking." Glumly, the Highwaywolf mooched off between the trees, muttering to itself.

At a signal from the King of Thieves, a score or so of heavily armed outlaws broke cover and came forward. "Hello," said Tym listlessly. He made an effort to pull himself together and try to be polite. "I suppose I should be grateful to you for saving my life."

There was a scrape of steel. A dozen swordpoints were suddenly at Tym's throat. Half a dozen arrows pointed unwaveringly at his heart.

"On the other hand," said Tym, "perhaps not."

A heavy wooden cudgel smacked into the back of Tym's head; the world exploded into flashing colours of pain, then faded into utter darkness.

A blindfold was whipped away from Tym's eyes. He blinked and looked around. He was in a building of some sort. The room was big with a high ceiling and dingy walls were just visible in the light of guttering candles. Tym struggled to his feet – and found himself surrounded by thirty or forty outlaws, all grinning and fingering metal things with sharp points. "Where am I?" he groaned.

His chief captor pricked Tym's throat with the point of his dagger. "At our hideout in Dun Indewood."

Tym was horrified. "You brought me back to the City? But I've been banished! I'm not supposed to be here! I'll get into trouble!"

"You're already in trouble, in case you 'adn't noticed."

Tym stared at his captor. "Who are you?"

The man gave him an evil leer. "I'm the King of Thieves, I am."

"The King of Thieves?" Tym's mind cleared a little more. "Oh, so you're a bunch of merry outlaws who call no man 'Master' and who live, free from care, in the greenwood, robbing from the rich and giving to the poor?" he said hopefully.

There were guffaws from all round the room. The King of Thieves grinned. "Partly right. Guess which part."

"Robbing from the rich and *not* giving to the poor?"

"Got it in one."

"Pleased to meet you."

"I don't fink so. On account of, I'm gonna slit yer weasand."

Alarm bells shrilled in Tym's head. He wasn't at all sure what his weasand was, but he was fairly clear that having it slit would not be good for his health. He gulped. He'd known that he was living on borrowed time from the moment that he was banished to the Forest. He'd just hoped that he could borrow a bit more of it.

"Dad, Dad, don't slit his weasand, Dad!"

Tym almost fainted with relief. Cutpurse Colyn! He remembered his meeting with the small thief on the streets of Dun Indewood. Colyn had called the King of Thieves "Dad" and he was sticking up for Tym. He had an ally!

"Don't you slit 'is weasand," repeated Colyn with shrill insistence. "I saw 'im first. I want ter do it." Tym groaned.

The King of Thieves shook his head firmly. "No, my son, you're too young."

Colyn bridled. "I ain't too young!"

The King of Thieves squatted down to look his son in the eye. "What would your poor old muvver say, may 'er soul rest in peace, if she thought I was lettin' yer go round slittin' weasands at your tender years?"

Colyn grew sulky. "Well, I bet I could slit 'is weasand as good as anyone else," he muttered.

The King of Thieves gave a sly smile to Tym. "On the uvver hand, s'posin' you was to do sumfing for us…?"

"Don't see what's so 'ard about slittin' some feller's weasand…"

"Like maybe we could come to some arrangement..."

"You never let me do nuffin'. I never 'ave any fun..."

"Colyn!" roared his father. "I'm sayin' as how we might not 'ave to slit 'is weasand."

Colyn scowled. "Well, I wish you'd make your bloomin' mind up!"

The King of Thieves rolled his eyes. "Kids!" He turned his attention back to Tym. "Well? Hows about it?"

Tym was thoroughly confused. "Hows about what?"

The King of Thieves leered at him. "You do sumfing for us, maybe I'll let yer go."

Tym felt a surge of hope. "And not slit my weasand?"

"That's the idea!" The King of Thieves clapped Tym on the back. "I 'eard about yer master makin' veg into gold..."

Tym shook his head. "Oh, but that was a trick. He didn't really..." He stopped in confusion. Telling the thieves he couldn't really provide gold for them probably wasn't the best possible survival strategy at this precise moment.

"Oh, I knows all that," said the King dismissively. "I had my people there at the WOSCAS, see? Young Colyn an' Captain Gorge..."

The captain waved a peg-arm. "Strike me feluccas, me hearties..."

"Shut up."

"Aye aye, Admiral."

"So I knows all about your little tricks." The King of Thieves wagged a finger playfully under Tym's nose. "Who's been a naughty boy, then? Tch tch tch."

Tym stared at him. "But then, what...?"

"…can you do for us? Well, this is how I sees it. If yer can move so fast yer becomes invisible, yer could be very useful to us. Slippin' past guards. Spyin' out the land. Nickin' stuff an' bringin' it to us. You catch my drift?"

Tym was starting to feel better. That made sense – he could be of use to the thieves. And then they wouldn't kill him out of hand. In fact, they'd have to treat him properly. He decided to push his luck. "You're taking a bit of a chance, aren't you?" he said daringly. "After all, if I'm as quick as you think I am, what's to stop me just taking off any time I feel like it? I could do it now! I could wriggle out of these bonds and be out of that door so fast you'd never see me go!"

"Well, yer could," conceded the King of Thieves, "if you was sure that yer could get to someplace where we'd never find yer. 'Cos I don't s'pose yer could keep movin' at that speed for ever, an' yer'd have to sleep sometime – 'ere in the City, or out there in the Forest, wiv every one o' my lads lookin' for yer wiv daggers in their fists an' cold murder in their hearts."

Tym gulped. "Good point, well made." He drew himself up to his full height. "I'll join you! Is there an oath or something?"

"Not so fast." The King of Thieves held up his hand. "We don't allow just any riff-raff into our band. You'll 'ave ter pass a test. And if you don't…"

Tym rolled his eyes. "Let me guess. You'll slit my weasand?"

The King of Thieves gave Tym a wink. "Got it in one… Again."

CHAPTER NINE

O f Plans, Potions and Possets.

Tym looked around at the outlaws, who were all grinning like wolves. "All right," he said nervously, "what do you want me to do?"

The King of Thieves stepped aside. There was a very small outlaw standing behind him. "Meet Big Jim. 'E's a brownie"
The brownie glowered at Tym. He was smaller than Colyn and looked like a tiny, wizened old man with knobbly knees, elbows and wrists, and a nose and ears that were much too big for its face.

Tym stared. "Big Jim?"

"Yeah!" The brownie's voice was menacing. "They calls

me that 'cos I'm so big. I daresay you noticed." Tym nodded quickly.

"Now then," said the King of Thieves, "as I expect you know, brownies reckon they're pretty fast. If a brownie lives in yer 'ouse, 'e'll clean the whole house from top to bottom, do all yer spinnin' an' weavin', milk yer cows, churn yer butter an' get yer breakfast while yer asleep, all for a saucer o' milk."

"Bloomin' starvation wages. Naked exploitation of the workers, I call it," muttered Big Jim. "Come the revolution, my brothers and I will demand saucers of cream all round. And chocolate fingers."

The King of Thieves groaned. "Stow it, Jim. We've all 'eard it. Anyway…" He turned back to Tym. "Point is, Jim 'ere 'as got to be pretty fast ter do in a night what'd take an army of servants a week. So yer test is – yer've got to nick that medallion wot Jim's wearin' round 'is neck…" With a frightful scowl at Tym, Big Jim held up a gold medallion, then thrust it back inside his jerkin. "An' yer've got to bring it to me before 'e knows it's missin'," the King concluded. "Got it?"

Tym nodded. It didn't sound too difficult. He didn't care how fast the brownie was, it wouldn't be a match for Whizzard speed.

Big Jim gave a contemptuous snort and turned his back on Tym. The grinning outlaws stood back to make a circle enclosing Tym and the brownie. Tym collected his wits. Here goes, he thought. Fast… faster…

There was a murmur from the watching outlaws. Tym was

flickering in and out of sight. He kept disappearing for a fraction of a second – then reappearing a few paces away. There... gone... there... gone...

Tym began to sweat. His eyes watered as he screwed them up with effort. Something was going terribly wrong. He made a supreme effort. Fast... fast...

The King of Thieves gave an impatient snort. "What's goin' on, then? Stop messin' about..."

Tym turned an anguished face to him. "I can't do it! The potion must have worn off. I'm not a Whizzard any more!"

"Oh dear, oh dear." Suddenly, Tym was once more surrounded by arrows notched to strings and blades poised ready to strike.

Slowly, the King of Thieves drew his dagger and stepped forward. "What a pity. Looks like we're gonna have to slit yer weasand after all..."

Tym held both his arms out in futile defence. "Wait!"

The King of Thieves paused. "Why?" he asked with mild interest.

"Because... because I *can* be a Whizzard again!" gabbled Tym. "There's this potion, you see. I made it. That's what turned me into a Whizzard and there's more of it in my knapsack!" He tore the frayed bag from his shoulder and held it out in front of him as a puny shield against the outlaws' arrows.

"More, eh?" The King of Thieves looked thoughtful. Nodding furiously, Tym fished out the bottle of Whizzard potion. "Well, that's very interestin'." The King gazed at Tym with a calculating expression. "You know what? I been finkin'. This potion o' yours, if it works on you, it'll work on anybody, right? So why don't yer just pour 'alf of it into this 'ere flask?" The King held up a flask which hung from his belt. "Then you take your 'alf, an' if yer not poisoned an' if it works on you, I can just drink the rest of it myself. That way, I can do the nickin' personally an' not need to trouble you wiv it. Cuttin' out the middle man, yer might say." He leered at Tym.

Tym hesitated – but he really had no choice. With a shrug, he held out the potion. The King took it and carefully decanted a good half of the liquid into his own flask which he then returned to his belt. He turned to Tym. "Righto, then. Bottoms up!"

"Not yet. There's one more ingredient. I'll need your knife."

Eyeing Tym distrustfully, the King passed him a wickedly sharp dagger. Grimacing, Tym jabbed the point into the ball of his thumb and let three drops of blood fall into his flask. The lilac vapour formed and all the outlaws went, "Ooooh!"

The King chuckled appreciatively. '"Now that's magic!"

Tym held his nose, lifted the potion to his lips, and swallowed. The King of Thieves gave him a savage grin. "All right, let's see if it's worked." He took his knife from his belt and hurled it across the room. It stuck, quivering, in the doorpost at the opposite end. "Let's see you go an' get that, lad."

He stood with his arms folded, grinning at Tym. Tym didn't move. After a while, the King of Thieves frowned. "Come on then, sunshine. Wotcha waitin' for?"

"Oh, sorry," said Tym. He handed the knife to the King. "Do you want me to do it again?"

The King of Thieves stared from the knife in his hand to the doorpost from which it had vanished, and back again.

Colyn crowed with triumph. "I *told* you, Dad! I *told* you!"

The King nodded slowly. "Very impressive. All right, now let's see you nick Big Jim's medallion..."

"You mean this medallion?" Tym held it out.

Big Jim gave a furious snort and fingered his neck, looking for the chain that was no longer there. He gave Tym a lethal glance and muttered something about, "Come the revolution..."

The King gave a hoarse chuckle. "That stuff's the business! Time I gave it a go." He reached for the flask at his side and his eyes widened. He felt along his belt. He looked on the ground all around where he'd been standing. Then he turned back to Tym, his face set in a furious scowl. "Where's my flask?"

"The one with the potion in it?" said Tym offhandedly. "I took it from you before I took the medallion from Big Jim. It's hidden."

The King's hunting knife sliced through the air where Tym had been standing a fraction of a second before, thudding into the wall a handspan above Big Jim's head. From behind the King, Tym said, "You should be more careful with that knife. You could have hurt somebody." All around the room, outlaws reached for arrows and drew their swords and daggers. Tym prepared to go back to Whizzard speed.

But the King gave a signal and his men relaxed. He held

one hand out, palm upwards. "Are you goin' to give me that potion?"

Tym knew the risk he was running, but his voice was steady. "No. If I did that, you'd be able to move as fast as me. So I wouldn't be able to escape you by going to Whizzard speed if you suddenly decided to slit my weasand because you didn't need me any more."

"Well, if you fink I'm just gonna take yer on a job an' just let yer go wanderin' off by yourself, you've got anuvver fink comin'." The King of Thieves glared at Tym. "Wot's to stop yer squealin' to the guards an' gettin' us all captured?"

Tym thought for a moment. The King of Thieves had a point. They were back to square one – unless... "I'll tell you what," Tym offered, "I'll give the other half of the potion to one of your band: but I get to choose which one."

The King clearly wasn't happy about this. He paced up and down for a long time before muttering, "All right. Deal. Who're you goin' to give the potion to?"

Without hesitation, Tym said, "Cutpurse Colyn."

Colyn punched the air with both fists. "Yeeeessssss!"

"Yer what?" The King let rip a frightful series of oaths. "That is bang out of order! I won't 'ave it. 'E's me own flesh an' blood, an' what's more..."

Tym was adamant. "A deal is a deal. I can choose whoever I like. Think about it. If I did betray you to the guards, Colyn could warn you before they arrived."

The King nodded slowly. "But we'd still need you because you're old enough and savvy enough not to wake the 'ole 'ouse by standin' on the cat tryin' to reach the door handle."

"Awwwww, Daaaad!" protested Colyn.

The King gave Tym a cold hard stare. "You, sunshine, are a clever, unscrupulous, crafty, scheming, untrustworthy, deceitful, slippery, two-faced, duplicitous little ratbag." Then he grinned and slapped Tym on the back. "Welcome to the Bruvverhood of Thieves!"

Later that night, as the outlaws sat around a sputtering fire, the King of Thieves outlined his plan to make use of Tym's Whizzard speed in their next caper.

"There's this necklace, right?" he said. "Up the Castle. Precious heirloom, sort of fing. It's a necklace made of Firestones. Priceless, it is. Belongs to one of the oldest families in the City, only the geezer in question an' 'is missus died of the plague a few years ago. The Firestones got passed on to their daughter, an' she's got them now. Or at least will 'ave until we nick 'em." The outlaws chuckled.

"Fing is, they're too well guarded to be got at by ordinary means. That's where our friend 'ere comes in." The outlaws darted glances at Tym. Some of them grinned. They were a lot friendlier now it looked at if Tym could help them rob people. "He goes in first an' drugs the guards' possets, see…"

One of the outlaws put up a hand. "What's a posset?"

A more well read outlaw answered, "It's a drink made from hot milk curdled with ale or wine…"

The King of Thieves nodded. "Right. So then he—"

"It's often flavoured with spices."

"Yeah, fank you, so then he—"

"It's popular as a bedtime drink and is sometimes used as a remedy for colds and similar minor ailments."

"Right, so then he—"

"The word possibly derives from the Old Indewoodian *poshote*, but its origin is— ow!"

The King of Thieves rubbed his stinging knuckles and went on, "So then he opens the doors an' goes in, and whizz, bosh and Bob's yer uncle! Any questions?"

For some time now, Tym had felt a horrible sinking feeling in the pit of his stomach. Now he asked quietly, "So who do the Firestones belong to?"

The King of Thieves looked surprised. "Didn't I say?" He shook his head sorrowfully. "Forget me own head next. They belong to Wossername. Lord Robat's granddaughter, 'er as was givin' out them WOSCAS – the Lady Zamarind."

Chapter Ten

How Tym and Colyn crept Upstairs, Downstairs, into the Lady's Chamber.

Tym and Colyn slipped down the dark corridors of the Palace of the High Lords. Faded tapestries lined the walls. Their embroidered images were shadowed into invisibility, though occasionally a hunting scene or Knyghtly coat of arms was illuminated by the glow of a candle whose flame never flickered. Guards, posted at every turn, stared impassive and unseeing as the Whizzard and his small companion sneaked past beneath their noses.

Tym cursed silently as he crept through the sleeping Castle. How could he possibly steal from Zamarind? He liked her! He wanted Zamarind to like him. But if he didn't help the thieves, Tym's life would be very short and unpleasant, and his final moments would probably involve a lot of agonised squealing. He had to find some means of making the plan go wrong in such a way that the thieves couldn't possibly blame him. But that was easier said than done.

The King's plan was simple enough. Once Colyn had dripped his blood into his own dose of potion and swallowed it, and Tym had shown him how to control his speed, the King had drawn an outline of their route on the dusty floor of their hideout. "There's two guards on the Lady Zamarind's chamber," he'd told them. "We've bin spyin' on their routine, see. Every night, one o' the maids takes them their possets. All you've got to do is slip some of this…" he held up a small bottle filled with cloudy liquid "…into their drinkies, an' hide while they go sleepy-byes. Then you nip in smartish, nick the sparklers an' drop 'em out o'the window where we'll be waitin'…"

The trouble was, the plan was so simple Tym had no idea how he could manage to make it go wrong. His mind still racing, he turned a corner… and stopped dead. Colyn clattered straight into his back. Tym bit back a yell of pain as the box Colyn was carrying swung round and fetched him a painful blow on the shin. "Mind where you're going!" he hissed furiously.

"It's yer own fault," Colyn snapped back. "Wot yer stopped for?"

"There's a maid coming down the corridor carrying two mugs," whispered Tym. "She must be taking them to Zamarind's guards."

"Well, you'd better go an' slip the knockout drops into 'em, hadn't you?" said Colyn.

Tym made 'shushing' motions with both hands. "Keep your voice down!"

"Wot for?" demanded Colyn truculently. "Nobody can 'ear us – or if they can, they won't know wot they woz 'earing. We're talkin' too fast for 'em to understand us. They'd probably think it was bats or insects or sumfing." He grinned. "Or ghosts." He held his arms above his head and made a face. "Whooooo!"

"Shutupshutupshutup!"

"Blimey, you aint 'alf a scaredy cat." Tym scowled menacingly at Colyn. "All right, all right, I'll keep quiet."

"And stop swinging that box about." Tym grimaced as he rubbed his sore shin. "What have you got in there anyway?"

Colyn gave him an unsettling grin and patted the box complacently. "Insurance."

"Well, stop hitting me with it. Look, stay here while I slip the sleeping potion into the drinks, right?"

"Then are you gonna slit 'er weasand?"

"No."

"Well, can I slit 'er weasand then?"

"No!" Tym rolled his eyes. "We won't need to slit anyone's weasand. Just stay here." He crept round the corner.

The maidservant was in the centre of the passageway, caught in mid-step. Her eyes didn't blink as Tym slipped down the corridor towards her and, hardly daring to breathe, unstoppered the bottle and began to pour the sleeping draught into the first mug.

"Here, posset, posset, posset."

Tym jumped a mile. He turned and glared savagely at Colyn who had crept up behind him and was now leaning against the wall, doubled up with laughter. "Hoooo, hoooo, hoooo," he chortled. "Would yer like a nice saucer of milk, posset? Hoooo, hooo. That's a good one, that is."

Tym grabbed him by the throat. "Will you shut up!"

"I told you, they can't 'ear us." Colyn pointed at Tym. "You should've seen your face. Hoooo, hoooo, hoooo…"

Tym leaned forward until he was nose-to-nose with the small outlaw. "Listen, cabbage-brain. Maybe they can't hear what we're saying, but if you were on guard in a Castle late at night and you heard strange noises, what would you do?" Colyn stopped laughing and Tym went on, "You'd call some other guards and investigate, wouldn't you? If your dad hears alarm bells coming from the Castle, I don't think he's going to be very pleased."

"All right, all right," muttered Colyn, "It was only a joke. Don't go on."

"Just keep quiet." Tym poured sleeping draught into the second mug. "Right. Now we hide and go to normal speed while the potion takes effect."

Colyn nodded. Crossing the corridor, he flung open an unguarded door. "In 'ere."

Tym was aghast. "What're you doing?" he demanded in a strangled yell. "That could be somebody's bedroom!"

Colyn gave him a scornful look. "I don't fink so. All Lord Robat's family 'as guards outside their rooms. No guards, no people. See?" Tym peered past him, into the gloom. Colyn was right. It seemed to be a storeroom, piled higgledy-piggledy with broken furniture and boxes. He slipped in, pulling Colyn through behind him and closing the door gently on both of them. Slow… slower… slowest…

Standing in the darkness, they heard the maid's footsteps recede. Then there was silence.

"Wot do we do now?"

"We wait for the sleeping potion to work."

There was a rustling noise. "What was that?" hissed Tym.

"What?"

"That noise?"

"Oh, that's just my box."

"Boxes don't rustle."

"No, I mean it's what's in the box."

"What have you got in there?"

Colyn's voice was sly. "That'd be tellin'. Anyway, 'ow long's it gonner take fer the potion ter work?"

"About five minutes."

"'Ow will we know when it's five minutes?"

Tym clenched his fists in the darkness. "Count to five hundred."

Pause.

"One – two – three – fower – five – six – seven – eight – nine – ten."

Pause.

"One – two – three – fower – five – six – seven – eight – nine – ten."

Pause.

"One – two – three—"

"What are you *doing*?" hissed Tym.

"Well, I never learned to count to five hundred. I thought I'd do it in bits."

Tym felt his head starting to ache. "Never mind. I'll count to five hundred and tell you when I've done it. All right?"

"All right."

Tym started to count under his breath. His voice fell into a steady rhythm. "...a hundred and forty, a hundred and forty-one, a hundred and forty-two..."

"'S a long time, five minutes, eh?"

"...A hundred and forty-three, a hundred and forty-four..."

"Why don't I nip out an' see what's goin' on?"

"*...A hundred and forty-five, a hundred and forty-...*"

"Dark in 'ere, innit?"

"Colyn!" hissed Tym. "Shut up!" He groaned. "Now you've made me lose count..." He sighed. "One, two, three..." At long last, Tym muttered, "...four hundred and ninety-nine, five hundred!"

Fast... faster... fastest... Moving at Whizzard speed again, Tym and Colyn slipped out of the storeroom and along the corridor. Tym checked the rough map the King of Thieves had given him. They were in this corridor here, so the Lady Zamarind's room should be... Tym stopped dead.

"Ow!" Tym swung round on Colyn. "I told you to watch that box..."

"Well, you keep stoppin'. Woss the matter now?"

Tym pointed. Outside the Lady Zamarind's door, two guards stood. They were bright-eyed and alert. The sleeping potion seemed to have had no effect on them whatsoever.

Colyn stared at them. "Ooer. Somethin' must 'ave gone wrong."

"Stay here!"

Tym raced back down the corridor, past the storeroom, round a corner… and skidded to a halt just in time to avoid a collision with the maidservant who had been carrying the possets, but who was coming, empty-handed, from quite the wrong direction. With a groan, Tym turned and sped back to Colyn. "Wrong possets!"

"Wot?"

Tym gestured impatiently. "We put the potion in the wrong possets. The maid's coming from another part of the Castle. The possets we thought were for the guards must have been for someone else."

Colyn shook his head. "Oooer! My dad's gonna be so mad at you…"

But a cheerful thought had struck Tym. He breathed a sigh of relief. "Oh, well," he said lightly, "that's it, isn't it? I mean, we can't possibly go through with the job now. I blame poor intelligence: nobody said anything about extra possets, but now we've used up all the sleeping potion and the guards are still awake, we'll…"

Colyn shook his head and went, "Tch tch tch."

Tym glared. "'Tch tch tch' what?"

"My old dad said you might try to worm your way out of this…"

"I'm not," Tym blustered. "But the guards are still awake and…"

"An' you're still a Whizzard, ain't yer? Puttin' the guards to sleep was only like an extra safety measure in case they 'eard somethin' while we was in the room. We now move to Plan K."

"Plan K?"

"Yes. The second plan."

"Shouldn't that be Plan B?"

"Yeah, well, I never learnt me alphabet neiver. Dad says, even if the guards is still awake, we can be in that room an' out again wiv the sparklers before they can spit. Right?"

Tym looked daggers at Colyn – but the small thief was right, there was no denying it. With a final, dubious glance at Colyn, Tym slipped between the guards to the Lady Zamarind's door and swung it carefully open. They both stepped through. Tym closed the door softly behind them, turned – and stood, staring about in consternation.

The King of Thieves hadn't said anything about *rooms*. He'd said the necklace was in the Lady Zamarind's *room*. But which one? The Lady Zamarind didn't live in a room. She lived in a lot of rooms.

All Zamarind's rooms were hung with drapes made of a sort of floaty stuff that looked as soft as thistledown and more expensive than a cartload of diamonds. There were lots of low-slung sofas and plump, shiny cushions (which Colyn bounced on until Tym dragged him away). There were marble pillars and white furniture with pink satin padding. Tym looked around in dismay. The necklace could be anywhere – and Tym didn't dare search. Amid such aggressive cleanness, he felt as if he would leave accusing black marks on anything he touched.

"Cor," said Colyn appreciatively, "Posh, innit?"

He and Tym wandered from the Receiving Room into the Blue Boudoir. Then they wandered through the Green, Yellow and Lilac Boudoirs. Each had its own bathroom. Then there was the Withdrawing Room, the Morning Room, the Afternoon Room, the Boring Bit Of The Day When It's Too Late To Go Out And Too Early To Go To Bed Room, the Supper Room, the Breakfast Room, the Dressing Room, the Undressing Room and finally, the Bedroom... Tym gave a muffled croak, shoved Colyn (who was straining to see over his shoulder) out and shut the door on the sleeping Zamarind as quickly as he dared.

Colyn stared at serried ranks of more drawers and cupboards than a single person could hope to fill in an entire lifetime, and whistled dubiously. "We'll never find the sparklers among all this lot."

Tym felt relief flood through him. "You're right. Well, well, well, what a pity, we'll just have to call the whole thing off—Where are you going?"

Colyn paused in his purposeful march towards Zamarind's bedroom door. "We'll never find it, so we'll 'ave to make 'er tell us where it is."

Tym's relief was replaced instantly with cold, sick horror. "You can't do that!"

"Yers I can – an' if she won't tell me..." Colyn drew his dagger and gave Tym an evil grin, "I shall just 'ave ter slit 'er weasand."

"You are not slitting the Lady Zamarind's weasand!"

Colyn was surprised. "Why not? Wot's it to you?" His eyes narrowed shrewdly and he gave a throaty chuckle. "You fancy 'er, don't you?" Tym was mortified to feel a blush spread across his face like a crimson stain. "I don't believe it!" Colyn pointed at Tym and chanted, "Tymmy fancies Zammy, Tymmy fancies—"

Tym made a dive for Colyn, who sidestepped neatly. Overbalancing, Tym slipped on a carelessly scattered scatter cushion. His feet shot from under him. He slammed headfirst into a marble pedestal on which was perched a rather tubby cupid, and passed out.

Colyn eyed the unconscious Whizzard with pursed lips. "Ought to be more careful," he said in disapproving tones. He calculated the trajectory of the toppling cherub and gave a malicious chuckle.

"Bull's-eye!" he said quietly and he sauntered towards the door of Zamarind's bedroom.

CHAPTER ELEVEN

H ow Zamarind looked Stunning, and received a Stunning Look.

A s the bedroom door slammed, Tym's eyes jerked open. His head hurt. Then the cupid fell on it and smashed, and it hurt a lot more. Tym clasped his aching skull with both hands and stifled a scream.

There was a shuffling of feet from outside in the corridor and a muttered conference. The blood in Tym's veins instantly turned to ice. The guards had heard the smash! He waited, not daring to breathe.

After a while, the muffled voice of one of the guards came through the door. "Is everything all right, m'Lady?"

Tym grabbed a fold of gauzy material and held it over his

mouth. In a high-pitched voice, he called, "Quite all right, thank you. I dropped something."

There was a long pause. Then, from outside, a slightly worried voice said, "Are you sure you're all right, m'Lady? You sound a bit... funny."

"I think I'm losing my voice. I've got a bit of a cold coming on. Achoo!" Tym added for authenticity. There was silence from the other side of the door. "Well, I'm going back to bed now. Nighty night," squeaked Tym desperately.

"Good night, m'Lady."

Tym waited, heart pounding, for a long time. The guard hadn't sounded convinced. But there was no noise from the other side of the door. At length Tym relaxed. As silence fell again, he realised that he could hear other voices. Two voices coming from behind the closed door of Zamarind's bedroom. How long had Tym been unconscious? What was Colyn up to? He might, at this very moment, be slitting the Lady Zamarind's weasand!

Throwing caution to the winds, Tym leapt for the door and flung it open. What he saw took him completely by surprise. The Lady Zamarind was sitting up in bed with her knees drawn up and her arms clasped across them. She didn't look in the least like someone in need of rescue.

Colyn was sprawled comfortably at the other end of the bed, with his box on the counterpane beside him. He was cleaning his fingernails with a dagger and chattering away like a starling.

"O' course, yer've gotta keep yer wits about yer when yer a thief – you know, always one jump ahead o' the guards—"

Colyn broke off as Zamarind turned towards the door, saw Tym, and clapped her hands. "Oh, goody!" she squeaked. "Another one."

"'Ello, Tymmy," said Colyn in a friendly voice. "I woz just explainin' wot it woz like, bein' a thief an' a fugitive from justice…"

"Never mind that!" Tym pointed an indignant finger at Colyn. "What are you doing in here?"

"Now, now, Tymmy, don't be jealous," said Colyn with an infuriating smirk. "Me an' Zammy 'ere was just getting acquainted."

Tym boggled. "*Zammy?*"

The Lady Zamarind gazed at Colyn with a look of proprietorial pride. "Isn't he *shocking*?!" she gushed happily. "All the people one normally meets say nothing but 'Yes, Milady' and 'No, Milady' and they never say anything funny at all, and they walk backwards out of whatever room one happens to be in. None of them talk to one properly or tell one interesting things." She gave Colyn an encouraging smile. "Tell me more about being a thief. One is so fascinated by low life."

Tym stared at her. "Is one? I mean, are you?"

Zamarind flounced in a way that gave Tym a momentary difficulty with his breathing. "Of course. One knows all about high life and it's very boring. When your little friend here woke me up, he threatened to slit my weasand." Zamarind gave a silvery laugh that made Tym's toes curl up inside his boots. "You see, there's so much one doesn't know. What is a weasand? How does one slit it? It's all frightfully intriguing."

Tym turned to Colyn. "So you've been in here, having a cosy little chat, while I've been getting bashed on the head by cupids."

"Fell on you, did it?"

"Yes!"

"Thought it would."

"Then I had to pretend to be the Lady Zamarind and tell the guards I'd dropped something." Zamarind giggled and clapped her hands. "I think they're getting suspicious," Tym went on, giving Zamarind a furtive, sideways glance. He took Colyn by the elbow and propelled him away from the bed. "You'd better get out there and keep watch."

"Why me?"

"Somebody's got to do it." Inspiration struck Tym. "You can watch the guards, and if they look like giving the alarm, you can slit their weasands!"

"Hey, yeah! Right!" A big grin spread all over Colyn's face. Then it faltered. "Fing is…" He bit his lip and gave Zamarind a strangely embarrassed look. "Fing is," he went on, dropping his voice confidentially, "wot I mean to say is… where is their weasands?"

Tym stared at him. "Don't you know?"

"Well, not *exackly*," said Colyn defensively.

"But you keep going on about slitting people's weasands! You've been doing it ever since I met you!"

"Yeah, well, that's just a fret, innit?"

"Just a threat?"

"Yeah, I mean, I know me old dad'd never actually let me slit nobody's weasand, so it don't matter if I sez I want to, 'cos 'e won't let me, an' it makes me look... yer know..."

"Tough?"

Colyn drew himself up to his full height. "Bloke's got to consider 'is reputation."

Tym shook his head. "Just go out of that door and if the guards look like raising the alarm, or somebody else comes, you can come in and tell me, all right?"

Colyn nodded cheerfully, sheathed his dagger and swung his box on to his hip. He gave Zamarind an outrageous wink. "See ya later, ducks."

Zamarind giggled. "Isn't he *frightful*?!" The she stared in amazement as Colyn disappeared. "Where's he gone?"

"It's a bit complicated. He's a Whizzard – like me – temporarily – I mean, he can move so fast you can't actually see him unless he stands still for a long time..."

Zamarind had stopped listening. She was gazing at Tym with an expression that mingled anger and disappointment. "*Whizzard*! I remember now. You're not a thief at all. You're that wizard's apprentice I had to banish the other day." Her eyes blazed. "How dare you come into my private apartments pretending to be a romantic brigand when you're nothing of the kind! What are you doing back here anyway?"

Tym quailed in the face of Zamarind's outburst. "Look, I'm sorry, I couldn't help it. The King of Thieves sent me to steal something..."

"Why didn't he send a proper thief?" demanded Zamarind indignantly.

Tym was nettled. "I am a proper thief!"

"No, you're not. You haven't the first idea of how to be a

thief. You don't even know what a weasand is."

Tym took a deep breath. "Look, I don't want to do this because I know it's wrong to steal and anyway I like you, but if I don't take your necklace of Firestones back to the King of Thieves, he really is going to slit my weasand, and he does know where it is. So please tell me where I can find the necklace."

Zamarind drew herself up proudly. "Oh, one couldn't possibly do that."

"But you've got to!" protested Tym. "I mean, I'm in your room, and it's two against one, and I'm a desperate cut-throat with a dagger and everything!"

"I know all that," said Zamarind with infuriating calm. "It's just that I can't tell you where the Firestones are. I would rather die than reveal the secret."

"You're bluffing," said Tym uncertainly. "I bet you don't mean that."

"I'm afraid I do. I wouldn't expect you to understand. It's an aristocracy thing. When my parents gave the Firestones to me for safekeeping, I promised to guard them with my life, so I will."

"But that's stupid!' Tym glared at Zamarind. "They're only *things*. They're only *stuff*. Why would you risk your life for a few glittery rocks?"

"I told you you wouldn't understand. It's not the Firestones that are important, it's my promise."

Tym shook his head wonderingly. "Are you always this stubborn?"

"I suppose so. Grandfather says that's why Daddy called

me Zamarind. You know – like tamarind – the fruit. Sweet and sour." Zamarind put her head on one side and gave Tym an uncertain, almost shy look. "Do you really?"

"Do I really what?"

"*Like* me?" Zamarind looked at her knees and twiddled her fingers. "You said you did."

Tym's mind felt like a cart that had lost three of its wheels. "Er... yes, well, of course I do. You're..." Tym gestured helplessly. "I mean... that is... but I don't suppose you... I mean, you must have lots of admirers."

"Oh, yes," said Zamarind offhandedly, "but I don't know if they really *like* me. For one thing, they're afraid of me, you see, and for another, I don't know whether they like me as a person or just fancy the idea of marrying Lord Robat's granddaughter and heir, so they can be richer and more powerful and all that."

Tym managed to pull himself together. He blushed ferociously and summoned up all his courage. "Well, I do like you," he said hesitantly. "I think you're the most wonderful—"

"Oy! Tym!"

Tym closed his eyes and clenched his fists. "Not now, Colyn!"

But Colyn was not to be put off. He grabbed Tym by the arm as Zamarind looked on in amazement. "Too right, now. When I got out there, one of the guards was missin', so I went to see where he'd got to: I thought he might 'ave just gone to the you-know-where or sumfing..."

Tym stared at him. "The you-know-where?"

"Yeah, the *you-know-where*." Colyn glanced at Zamarind

and coloured. "For a you-know-what. You *know*." Zamarind giggled and ducked her head behind her knees.

Enlightenment dawned. "Oh!" said Tym. "Had he?"

"No! He'd gone to tell the uvver guards somethin' was up! I listened at the door. They're on their way 'ere now!"

Tym gazed at Colyn in consternation. "What? We've got to do something!"

Colyn's face was grim. "Don't you worry, I've thought of everyfing." He patted the box slung at his waist. "Told you I 'ad insurance."

"What d'you mean, insurance?" Tym eyed Colyn's box with sudden apprehension. "What have you got in there?"

"Cockatrice." Colyn shook the box violently. "I'll just make sure 'e's in a bad temper..."

Tym gazed at Colyn in horrified disbelief. "A cockatrice? Are you talking about the legendary beast, hatched by a lizard from a cockerel's egg, with the power to kill any living creature with a glance?'

Colyn nodded. "The very same. I wasn't aware there was any uvver sort."

The Lady Zamarind looked from Tym to Colyn with an expression of concern. "Don't you think this could get a bit out of hand?" she asked nervously.

"Out of hand?" Tym pointed a quivering finger at Colyn. "You're mad! Those beasts are deadly!"

"I know that, dont I?" said Colyn grimly. "Them guards bursts in 'ere an' *zappo*!"

"But they're people!"

"They're guards. We're thieves. That's the way it is. We

get them before they get us. It's nothing *personal*."

"You can't do it! I won't let you!"

"Try an' stop me. You're nothin' but a traitor, you are. You never wanted this plan to work in the first place an' now you're just tryin' to…"

Colyn never finished his sentence. The door slammed open and half a dozen burly guards piled in, weapons drawn. After that, things happened very quickly.

The men charged. Colyn swung to face them, and opened the box. Tym cried, "No!" and lunged for the box, knocking it out of Colyn's hands. It fell on the bed.

Horror robbed Tym of movement as the cockatrice stalked out with rigid, jerky movements, hissing like a kettle. It blinked once, then turned its deadly gaze on the nearest person present – the one actually *in* the bed.

Tym gave a howl of despair and went to Whizzard speed. Even so, he was not fast enough. The cockatrice's stare shot from its eyes in two pulsing beams of light. Tym lunged forward, keeping one eye on the cockatrice and one on the murderous beams of light. They were moving at a speed that made Tym feel as though he were swimming in treacle.

Faster and faster.

Nearer and nearer.

Tym reached out for the terrible little lizard… but he was too late. The cockatrice's deadly stare had already connected with the shocked eyes of the Lady Zamarind.

CHAPTER TWELVE

How the Plan was a Washout, the Thieves were Washed Up and the Dreamwalker almost Washed His Hands of Tym.

Tym snatched the cockatrice. It blinked, shutting off its stare. Then it went limp. Some instinct made Tym snatch his hand away from the creature's still body. It hung in the air and began to glow, then shrivel, as if consumed by inner fires. Distractedly, Tym remembered that a cockatrice died after an attack with its killing stare, like a bee that has used its sting.

Then the cockatrice vanished in a puff of smoke. Tym blinked and looked around. The guards were suspended in mid-charge. With raised weapons, they were frozen in the act of rushing at Tym, wearing expressions that chilled his blood. Two had seized Colyn, who evidently had not had the presence of mind to go to Whizzard speed.

Even as the thought came to Tym, Colyn's body twitched into movement. He struggled in the guards' motionless grasp. "Leave go, can't you?" he complained. He turned to Tym. "Don't just stand there gawpin'. Get 'em off me!" Tym stared at him, breathing hard. "Oh, come on!" protested Colyn. "Wot's the matter?"

"You…" Tym struggled for words. "You… halfwit! You maniac! What did you want to bring a cockatrice for?"

"Well, it would've worked all right if you 'adn't knocked it out of me 'ands!" Colyn turned an unusually troubled face towards the still figure on the bed. "Is she all right?"

"I shouldn't think so!" Tym's voice was unsteady. "I didn't get to the cockatrice in time."

"Well, if you got to it quick, maybe she didn't get the full dose. Maybe she ain't dead."

Tym pulled at his hair. "How can I tell? When I'm at Whizzard speed, *everybody* looks like that! And if I go back to normal speed to find out, those guards will chop me to bits and then tell me I can appeal against being brutally dismembered provided I do it in writing within fourteen days." He shuddered.

"Well, we'd best get away from 'ere then." Colyn started wriggling again. "Come on, be a mate, 'elp us out of this!"

Tym glared. "I should leave you for the guards."

"Don't be like that!" Colyn's bluster and bravado disappeared. "I never meant to 'urt 'er. She an' me was gettin' on nicely. I thought she was all right, for a toff."

Tym sighed. "Oh, all right!"

With some difficulty, he pried the guards' clutching fingers away from Colyn's arms and the small thief stepped out of their grasp. "Ta," he said. "Now we'd better find my dad an tell 'im to get the lads out of 'ere smartish. I don't fink Lord Robat's goin' to be a happy bunny when he finds out about this."

Tym didn't argue. What else could they do? He and Colyn inched round the charging guards, out into the corridor. As they pelted through the Castle, everywhere they saw the signs of alarm and sudden awakening. More guards were charging down corridors. Some were shrugging mail shirts over their heads; some were buckling on armour; others were caught in mid-hop as they got both feet down one leg of their chain-mail britches.

Candle flames were drawn into horizontal streaks by the wind of their passing. Everywhere, doors were opening. Servants and officials in nightclothes were in various stages of emerging from their rooms. As they whizzed through the Castle, Tym and Colyn had to swerve to avoid Lord Robat, who was coming through the door of his rooms, pulling a cloak on over his nightdress and holding, for some reason, a chamber pot which he brandished like a weapon.

On they raced, down the Grand Stair, across the deserted Great Hall, through the Ceremonial Doorway and down the steps to the courtyard, where puzzled guards were just beginning to turn towards the commotion at the Palace. They pelted across the courtyard and into the shelter of a hut belonging to the stonemasons who, in daylight hours, worked on the Castle walls. The King of Thieves, Big Jim and Captain Gorge were standing at the window, staring out with worried expressions.

Tym fought to control his ragged breathing, and the frantic pounding of his heart. Slow… slower… slowest…

The outlaws whirled round as Tym and Colyn popped into view behind them. Now at normal speed, Tym could hear the ringing of alarm bells and shouts coming from the Castle. Lights were springing up at every window.

The King grabbed Tym by the front of his tunic and half-lifted him from the ground. "Wot's 'appened?" he demanded in a hoarse whisper. "You've gone an' woke the 'ole shebang! Can't yer even commit a single little robbery wivout messin' it up?"

Tym tried to twist free. "No time to explain – you've got to get your men away, now!"

"'Ave yer got the Firestones?" Tym shook his head. The King of Thieves gave a snort of derision. "No problem then. If there's nuffink missin' they'll go on shoutin' for a bit an' then post extra guards an' go back to bed, an' we can sneak out quiet-like."

"No!" howled Tym. "You don't understand! They're going to come looking for you. Colyn had a cockatrice and—"

The King's eyes widened. He gave his son an appalled stare. "You never!"

Colyn scuffed his toe in the stone dust on the floor. "Sorry, Dad."

"'Ow many times 'ave I told you never to go on a job tooled up?! An' a cockatrice! That's loaded for troll, that is!"

His jaw dropped. "Don't tell me it got somebody!"

With tears in his eyes, Tym nodded. "The Lady Zamarind."

"Oh, strewf! Oh, that's perfect, that is!" Beads of sweat sprang up on the King of Thieves' brow. "They'll hunt down every thief in the City! They'll boil us all in oil an' burn us at the stake an' 'ang us by the froat until we're sorry!" The King turned to Captain Gorge and Big Jim: "Listen. Tell the lads to get out. Now. Anyway they can. Every man fer 'imself. Meet back in the Forest. Got it?" Big Jim nodded grimly and raced away with Gorge hopping desperately in his wake. The King turned a scowling face on Tym and Colyn. "You'd better 'ope you don't get out of this alive, 'cos if you do, I'm gonna kill you!" He slipped out of the door and into the shadows.

"Come on." Colyn disappeared.

Tym stood blinking for a moment – then went to Whizzard speed and followed Colyn out of the door. He grabbed the small thief by the arm. "What about your dad?"

Colyn shook him off. "It's a bit late for you to go worryin' about my dad now," he said in a shrill voice. "Anyway, you 'eard what 'e said. Every man fer 'imself. All thieves know what that means." He turned to go.

Tym stopped him. "But we could help him escape?"

"'Ow?" demanded Colyn savagely. "'E can't go at Whizzard speed. 'E'd only slow us down an' then we'd all be captured. Tha's what 'every man for 'imself' means. 'E'll just 'ave to take 'is chances. So will you. So will I."

Their journey back to the thieves' hideout was a nightmare. The alarm bells from the Castle seemed to have roused the whole City. When they understood what had happened, the townsfolk had instantly armed themselves with anything sharp that came to hand and organised themselves into bands of vigilantes. Lady Zamarind was popular.

The citizens' militia hampered the guards quite as much as they helped them; they seemed to be everywhere, rushing down every street with blazing torches. As they made their way through the City, Tym and Colyn came across many bands that had captured thieves and were hauling them through the streets to the Castle. Big Jim was one of the captives. Tym and Colyn, still moving at Whizzard speed, tried to prise the outlaws free, but their captors' grip was too strong and there were simply too many of them. Eventually, weeping with frustration, they gave up.

Colyn led the way back to the old warehouse that was the thieves' City base – only to find it crawling with Lord Robat's guards. At last, they found their way into an abandoned house in the heart of The Grumbles, the lowest of Dun Indewood's low-rent districts. Colyn sat on the bare boards in a corner of the attic and buried his head in his arms, shivering.

Tym felt helpless and guilty. In an attempt to comfort Colyn, he said, "At least we didn't see your dad being captured. Maybe he got away."

Colyn raised a tear-stained face. "Maybe," he said in a voice that was meant to be proud but held the hint of a sniffle. "I reckon 'e'll diddle 'em. 'E's a slippery customer, my dad." His face crumpled again. "But look at all the lads as got took! An' them that is 'idin' might still get took. There's a lot of people lookin' for 'em." He shook his head sorrowfully. "Look at it any way yer like, it's a bust-up, this is. A right royal bust up! An' it's partly down to me."

"*Partly?*" Tym spluttered indignantly. "It was *all* your fault!"

Colyn bridled. "Oh yeah? Oo put the posset in the wrong mugs?"

"Who let the cupid fall on my head and alert the guards?"

"Oo knocked the cockatrice onter the bed?"

"Who took the cockatrice in the first place?"

Colyn shook his head sorrowfully. "Wot's the point in arguin'? Me dad should've slit yer weasand when 'e 'ad the chance." The small thief buried his face again.

Tym slumped to the floor. Exhausted by a sleepless night, a long day, and the horrors of the failed attempt to steal the Firestones, he slept.

Tym found himself on a familiar barren plain. The Dreamwalker was there, but this time he stood outlined against the sky, his back towards Tym. His head was tilted upwards as if he was gazing across infinities of space.

Without turning, the Dreamwalker said, "*Do you see where your folly has led you?*"

Tym didn't reply. His eyes filled with tears.

"*Will you now use the gift I have given you for such a base purpose? To steal and deceive? To creep and skulk in corners,*" *and take what is not rightfully yours?"*

"What else could I do?" Tym burst out. "*The thieves would have killed me if I hadn't helped them!*"

The Dreamwalker began to fade. In a voice, as cold as rime on a frozen pond he said, "*You have failed me. You have failed yourself.*"

Tym dropped to his knees and held out his arms in supplication. "*Dreamwalker!*" he cried. "*I know I have failed you! But I beg you, speak to me now! Tell me what I must do!*"

There was no reply. Dream-tears fell from Tym's eyes and splashed into the arid dust of the plain. "*I should never have agreed to help the thieves. What happened to the Lady Zamarind was my fault. I know that. But I want to make it right! Help me!*"

His only answer was silence.

"*I promise you, whatever you tell me to do, I shall do it, if only it will help her. If she can still be helped.*" Tym's voice cracked. "*At least tell me if she is alive or dead.*"

For an immeasurable time, there was silence. Then a voice, as faint as the sighing of the night wind, whispered, "*See...*"

Slowly, the shadowy figure of the Dreamwalker materialised again. It stepped aside – and there was Zamarind, sitting on the dry, dusty floor of the desert. Her eyes were wide and frightened.

Tym cried her name and stepped forward. She turned to him and, in a voice hollow with dread and desolate with loss, cried, "*What is this place? What have you done to me?*" Then

127

she fell face down on to the cold, comfortless earth and sobbed bitterly.

"*I'm sorry,*" whispered Tym. "*I'm sorry, I'm sorry.*" There didn't seem to be anything else to say.

"*She has being only in my world now,*" whispered the Dreamwalker, looking down on the frail figure with compassion, "*in the world of dreams. She is not alive. Nor is she dead. She is… lost.*"

"*But if she isn't dead, I can still help her!*" In the black ashes of Tym's despair, a spark of hope rekindled. "*Tell me what to do!*"

"*You will see your way, if you choose to take it. You must return to the Castle.*" Tym shook his head dumbly. That was madness. "*You must!*" the Dreamwalker insisted. "*Only thus can you learn what you must do.*"

The figure of the Dreamwalker stooped and gathered Zamarind into its cold embrace before beginning to fade. Tym opened his mouth to call on it to wait and tell him more…

Instead, he was jerked awake. Colyn was shaking him by the shoulder. Daylight was pouring through numerous gaps in the roof.

Tym groaned. "You again. Why don't you go away?"

"Go where?" demanded Colyn. "There's nowhere safe fer us in Dun Indewood, not now they know we've killed the Lady Zamarind…"

"She's not dead."

"…An' she treated me decent, for a toff, an'— Wot did you say?"

"She's not dead. Don't ask me how I know. But she will be dead soon if I don't do something to help her."

Colyn thought for a moment, then stood up decisively. "We'd better get on with it then."

Tym stared. "We?"

"A bloke's got 'is responsibilities," said Colyn loftily. "You say yer gonna 'elp the Lady Zamarind. Fair enough. But yer not goin' on yer own." Colyn's mouth twitched into its more familiar mischievous grin. "I'm comin' wiv yer."

CHAPTER THIRTEEN

How Tym and Colyn found a Cure and
Went to the Dogs.

"**I**t's weird this, innit?"

Tym marched purposefully towards the Castle, ignoring Colyn who was trailing behind him like a small, scruffy dog. "I mean," Colyn went on, "all these people, still as stachers."

"They're not statues," snapped Tym. "They're moving at a normal speed. Just getting on with their lives. Lucky old them." He kicked moodily at a pebble, which left the toe of his boot and hung in the air, as motionless as the inhabitants of Dun Indewood all around them.

"I know that, don't I?" Colyn's voice was aggrieved. "All I'm sayin' is, that's wot they look like. Jus' a load o' stachers:

there's stachers o' people walkin', an' stachers o' people eatin', an' stachers o' people tradin' an' payin' for wot they bought wiv coins wot they're takin' out o' their completely defenceless an' unprotected purses..."

"Colyn!" Tym swung round and pointed an accusing finger at the small thief, who swiftly hid the sharp knife he'd drawn behind his back. He gave Tym a guilty look. "Listen," Tym said harshly, "I never wanted you to come with me in the first place and I only agreed on one condition. What was it?"

"Yeah, but there's all these purses just danglin' there, beggin' to be cut an—"

"*What was it?*"

In sulky tones, Colyn muttered. "No cuttin' o' purses or pickin' o' pockets while we're movin' at Whizzard speed."

"Right. So you can put that gent's purse back where you found it."

"You're nothin' but a wet blanket, you are."

"We're in enough trouble already," Tym pointed out, "and we've got a job to do, remember? We're supposed to be going up to the Palace to find out what's happened to the Lady Zamarind. So forget about pinching people's purses and come on, if you're coming!" Tym turned on his heel and strode off, weaving through the immobile townsfolk, without a backward glance.

"Oooooouuuuuuwwwwwwwlllllllll."

A long, wavering, melancholy howl echoed around the City. Tym stopped dead in his tracks, the hairs on the back of his neck tingling. "What was that?"

"What's the matter with you now, mummy's boy?" Colyn

scoffed. "It's only a little doggie."

Tym turned a puzzled face to Colyn. "Is that right? In that case, how come we can hear it?"

Colyn paused mid-scoff. He licked his lips nervously. "Hey, you're right. If it was 'owlin' at normal speed, we shouldn't be able to— Oh, blimey. No, he couldn't 'ave. It's too soon."

Tym groaned. "I'm not going to like this, am I?"

"Well," said Colyn hesitantly, "there've been rumours, ever since 'Umfrey the Boggart come to work in the City. He's got like progressive ideas, see…"

"What sort of ideas?" Tym resumed walking, casting nervous glances around him.

"Like criminal detectorin'. Fing is, if a thief robs yer, an' you shout 'Stop, thief!', either 'e gets caught or 'e doesn't. If 'e gets caught 'e's guilty, if 'e doesn't, 'e's got away wiv it. Simple, see? But that's not good enough for Mr Clever Boggart. 'Im an' the Runemaster 'ave started detectorin' and they sometimes know who's gonna get robbed, so they're watchin' 'em to catch the robber. An' if they don't know about it before, they ask the Runes 'Oo robbed so-an-so an' where is 'e 'idin?' an' then they kick 'is door down in the middle o' the night an' drag 'im off to the Castle dungeons."

"Too bad," said Tym unsympathetically.

"Yeah, but that's not all. There's so many robberies 'appenin', an' the Inquestigators can't be everywhere at once, so the word on the streets is that 'Umfrey's been plannin' to bring in extra 'elp."

"Oooooouuuuuuwwwwwwwlllllllll."

Again, the terrible cry rose above the low hum of City life. It sounded closer this time. Tym stared apprehensively at Colyn. "What sort of help?"

"'Elp from the Forest," said Colyn glumly. "Supernatural 'elp, you might say."

Tym closed his eyes. "Go on."

Colyn shrugged. "Word is, 'e's been after a pack o' wish hounds."

"Oooooouuuuuuwwwwwwwwlllllllll." For the third time, the howl rose above the City: to Tym and Colyn it no longer sounded mournful, but threatening and full of sinister purpose.

"W-w-w-wish hounds?" stuttered Tym.

"Like I said, it's only a rumour."

Tym stared about wildly. "Where are they? Can you see them?"

Colyn shook his head worriedly. "No, well, we wouldn't, see, on account of them bein' invisible. They're phantoms."

"Phantoms?" Tym's eyes boggled.

"Yeah. Definitely of the spectral persuasion, yer actual wish hounds," said Colyn knowledgeably. "Yer can't see 'em. No heads, no eyes, no noses…"

"Then how do they smell?" asked Tym.

Colyn couldn't help grinning. "Terrible!"

Tym clenched his fists. "If you've been making all this up just for a cheap laugh…"

"I'm not! Straight up! And I don't know 'ow they can smell us out." Colyn shrugged. "All I know is, they live in the Forest an' 'unt in packs. An' once they've got yer scent, yer a gonner. Follow yer anywhere."

"But we're moving at Whizzard speed," Tym protested. "How can they be tracking us at the rate we're going?"

Colyn shrugged. "'Ow can they be trackin' us wiv no noses? 'Ow can they make them 'orrible 'owling noises wiv no mouths? They're magical creatures, I told yer. Wiv phantom noses to smell yer an' phantom ears to 'ear yer an' phantom teef to bite yer…"

"And phantom tails, I suppose, to wag when they want to go for phantom walkies?"

"You won't fink it's so funny when they get yer. Like I said, once they've got our scent…"

"…they'll follow us anywhere," concluded Tym. He grabbed Colyn's arm and set off at a run. "In that case, we haven't got much time."

They pelted through the still, crowded streets until they came to the Palace. Several times more they heard the strange howls of the wish hounds as they cast about the City, trying to pick up the scent of the fugitives. Tym and Colyn had just reached the drawbridge when the sound from the pursuing Hounds changed. Their howls became frenzied and eager, and the noise was getting nearer.

"They've got the scent!' moaned Colyn. "Oh, lumme…"

"Come on!" Tym dragged the whimpering thief through the corridors, still thronged with distraught-looking servants and grim-faced guards. Sidestepping these obstructions, they raced on until they came to the Lady Zamarind's rooms where they screeched to a halt, facing a scene to melt a heart of stone.

Zamarind was in bed, her dark hair spread out across the pillows that propped her up. Her eyes were open. Old Lord Robat, weeping, was holding her hand. The Runemaster stood on the other side of the bed, with Humfrey the Boggart at his side. Zamarind's old Nurse sat on a stool near the door, frozen in mid-bawl and holding a dripping handkerchief (half a dozen drips were inching their way towards the floor) to her eyes. All around the room, in attitudes of grave concern, stood the senior wizards and witches of Dun Indewood.

Colyn made a face. "What do we do now? We still can't find out how she is! The moment that lot see us, they'll start yellin' for the guards!"

"I've got an idea." Tym selected a wizard of about his own build and picked the unresisting figure up in a fireman's lift. "Find one your own size and bring him along…"

"Is that the best you could do?" Tym directed a critical stare at Colyn in his wizard disguise, who took instant offence.

"None of them was my size," he complained. "I dun my best." The wizard's pointy was slipping down over Colyn's eyes. The hem of his robe dragged along the ground and, even with the sleeves rolled up, only the tips of his finger were visible.

Tym checked his own robes. "Well, we can't be too choosy. Those wish hounds could be here any minute:

we've got to find out what we need to know and get out of here." He stepped over the unmoving bodies of the two wizards he and Colyn had carried out of Zamarind's room. They were lying on the floor in their underwear, bound and gagged.

Taking a deep breath, Tym, followed by Colyn, re-entered Zamarind's bedchamber where they took their victims' places among the other wizards. Slow... slower... slowest...

The scene came to life. All the wizards were arguing at once.

"Gentlemen!" The Runemaster's authoritative tones cut across the gabble. There was a high-pitched cough from one side of the room. "And Ladies," the Runemaster continued smoothly, bowing to the leader of a coven of witches. "These arguments are getting us nowhere! I am ready to entertain any suggestions that may bring about the recovery of poor Lady Zamarind."

At this, Lord Robat buried his face in his hands and the Nurse howled louder than ever. The wizards and witches shuffled their feet.

The Great Bozo said, "I could saw her in half."

There was a silence. Everyone looked at him.

"And would that aid her recovery?" asked the Runemaster.

The Great Bozo blushed. "Well, on past form, probably not."

"Are there any sensible suggestions?" continued the Runemaster.

Tym listened avidly. But the responses were disappointing. Zakkary the Unpleasant offered to scare the Lady Zamarind awake (or into fits, whichever came first). LeRoy the Magnificent said that he could create an illusion that the Lady Zamarind was well. "Of course, she won't actually be well," he said offhandedly, "but you'll hardly notice the difference." The Nurse howled louder and Lord Robat gave LeRoy the Magnificent such an unfriendly look that he shut up.

Gerimee the Miraculous raised one hand tentatively. "Er… excuse me…"

"I could turn her into a frog," offered one of the wishes

The Runemaster stared at the witch. "Would that do her any good?"

"No, but you could put her to live in the well and rent out her rooms."

Zamarind's Nurse had hysterics.

Gerimee the Miraculous tried again. "Excuse me…"

The Runemaster turned to Lord Robat, his shoulders slumped in defeat. "I am sorry, my Lord. It appears your wizards have nothing to offer. Perhaps your doctors…"

"Doctors!" quavered Lord Robat distractedly. "Useless, the whole pack of 'em! Worse than you lot! They wanted to plaster my granddaughter all over with leeches. Leeches! Buffoons and halfwits every one! Haven't you got any ideas? You!?" His finger jabbed at Tym.

All eyes turned to Tym. At the same moment, a chorus of howling sounded just outside the Palace, causing Tym to jump like a startled deer.

"Don't bounce about like that, man!" Lord Robat snapped. "This is a sickroom, not a gymnasium! What's your name?"

"Er… Zippo the Swift…"

"Well, have you got any bright ideas?"

"Erm… I'm afraid I must have missed a bit of the discussion," said Tym hesitantly. "How is the Lady?"

The Runemaster groaned. "Hast thou not been listening? The Lady Zamarind was stunned by a cockatrice. For some reason we cannot guess, she seems to have escaped the full effects of the creature's stare. Nevertheless, its baleful influence grows upon her and she will die…" At this point, the Runemaster was forced to break off until the howls of grief from the Nurse had subsided. "…unless a cure can be found. Alas, there is no one among thy brethren here who can tell what that cure might be."

Gerimee the Miraculous said, "Excuse me…"

The Runemaster gave him a furious glare. "For pity's sake, what is it?"

Gerimee said humbly, "I think I may have a cure."

"Ooooooouuuuuuuwwwwwwwwlllllllll." The noise was so close it was obvious that the wish hounds were somewhere inside the Palace. Colyn rolled his eyes at Tym; he looked ready to bolt. Tym shook his head – they couldn't leave now, not when they might be about to learn how to cure Zamarind! Tym looked around distractedly, and noticed that Humfrey was watching them both with an appraising stare.

All the wizards were now looking at Gerimee, a small, pasty-faced wizard who looked as if he got too many ideas and not enough exercise. Nervously, he said, "In a spellbook of the Great Mage Abna Cadava, I found a spell… that is, a potion… to cure the effects of partial exposure to the stare of a cockatrice. Of course, such an event is very rare because the condition is nearly always fatal to begin with, but Abna insists that it will work."

Lord Robat faced him eagerly. "And can you make this potion?"

"Oh, yes," said Gerimee matter of factly. "Any competent Spellbinder could. But while most of the ingredients are really rather commonplace, there is one essential element that is so rare I have never heard of anyone possessing it."

"And what might that be?" asked the Runemaster.

"A single scale from the tail of the Cumhera."

There was a moment's shocked silence. Then the door burst open and pandemonium reigned as the bedroom became suddenly full of noise and invisible hairy bodies. Tym turned to flee and found himself knocked to the ground. Invisible or not, the wish hounds' power was irresistible. Tym went to Whizzard speed – and it made no difference. The Runemaster and his companions froze: not so the wish hounds, which merely growled. Tym reverted to normal speed and slumped to the floor in defeat.

"Get this perishin' 'ound orf of me!" Dimly, Tym heard Colyn's voice raised in complaint. "Oh, gor... it's dribblin' phantom slobber all over me – an' its phantom breff smells like an ogre's underpants!"

"Well, well, well." Humfrey the Boggart clicked his fingers and Tym felt the weight on his back lift. The wish hounds seemed to have withdrawn a few paces, but as he sat up, Tym was very aware that they were still very much on the alert, and any false move would have their teeth snapping at his throat. The fact that he couldn't see their teeth wasn't a comfort.

The boggart gave Tym and Colyn a mirthless grin. "Look what the dogsh have dragged in. Shpill it, shweetheartsh. You got some explainin' to do."

CHAPTER FOURTEEN

Of Snags and Scales and Sea Dog's Tales.

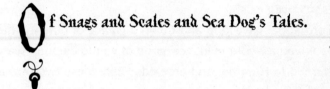

"And then the cockatrice stared at the Lady Zamarind and I tried to stop it, only I wasn't quick enough, and she looked into the stare before I could reach it, and that's how she ended up like this, and then we had to get away," Tym finished miserably.

He looked up into the stony faces of the assembled wizards and witches. Judging from their reaction to his story, they weren't impressed. The two wizards whose robes Tym and Colyn had stolen (now untied and reclothed) were giving the prisoners particularly nasty looks. It was clear that if they had their way, being turned into cockroaches and stamped on would be the best that Tym and Colyn could hope for.

The Runemaster looked thoughtful. "So thou brokest the contact between the cockatrice and the Lady Zamarind after a very short space of time – a millionth of a second, perhaps. That is why she did not die immediately."

Humfrey looked downcast. "I don't shee how thish does ush any good. The only hope we've got of curing the Lady ish to find the shcale of a creature that no one hash ever sheen, and hardly anybody hash even heard of, and that probably doeshn't even exisht."

Lord Robat gave Tym and Colyn a glance of pure loathing. "Thank you for your evidence, good of you to come forward." He turned to Humfrey and ordered, "Take these two out, like a good feller, and hurt them very, very much. Torture them nigh unto death, flog them within an inch of their lives, have them hanged, drawn, burnt at the stake and torn apart by wild horses, and then see that the remains are flung into the Forest to be devoured by wild beasts, if you would be so kind." Tym felt cold shivers run up and down his spine.

Colyn looked shocked. "Be fair, yer Lordship. First offence!"

Humfrey frowned. "I'm not sure that'sh wishe, my Lord."

Lord Robat's brow furrowed. "Wishe? Oh, you mean wise."

"Exshactly. Let'sh look at all the poshibilities before we do anythin' too hasty, whaddaya shay?" Lord Robat looked bewildered. Humfrey rolled his eyes. "Hey, Runie, tell ush more about thish whatshishname."

"The Cumhera?" The Runemaster pondered. "Well, it hath

a lion's head, a goat's body and a serpent's tail, and it breathes fire. And it's very quick."

"How quick?"

"So quick that no one has ever seen it."

"How do you know what it looksh like if no one has ever sheen it?"

The Runemaster said loftily, "That concerns the Lore of Wizards, which surpasses your understanding."

Humfrey grinned. "You always shay that when I ashk you shomething and you don't know the anshwer." The Runemaster gave Humfrey a quelling look which the boggart ignored. "Sho, what it boilsh down to ish, nobody can shee, much lessh catch thish creature because it'sh sho fasht."

"Correct."

"Nobody, that ish, except shomeone as quick as the creature itshelf." Humfrey looked pointedly at Tym and Colyn.

Lord Robat snorted. "Are you suggesting that the task of obtaining the scale from the Cumhera that might cure my granddaughter should be given to these two... malefactors... who caused her plight in the first place?" Tym's heart began to pound with renewed hope.

Humfrey scratched his ear. "Way I shee it, you don't have much choice." He turned to Tym. "I take it there ishn't any more of thish Whizzard potion of yours?" Tym shook his head. "Sho we can't jusht confishcate it and give it to shomeone elshe."

One of the witches offered, "I could turn him into a frog and sit on him until he agreed to make some more." She leered at Tym, who calculated the probable tonnage of her bottom and shivered at the thought.

"Tempting," said Humfrey with a nasty grin at Tym, "but it wouldn't work. He told ush he'd used up all the ingredientsh and the Wizard Herbit hashn't got any more. It took a Whizzard to get the Lady Zamarind into thish messh: the way I shee it, it'sh going to take a Whizzard to get her out of it."

Tym forced himself to stand upright. "My Lord," he said to Robat in a voice that quavered only a little, "I know that it is my fault that this terrible fate has befallen the Lady Zamarind. I will do everything I can to make amends. You may, if you will, have us brutally put to death..." ("Oy!" protested Colyn, "Speak for yerself!") "...but if you do, your granddaughter will certainly die."

Lord Robat shot an enquiring look at the Runemaster, who sighed. "It seems there is no help for it, my Lord. These two scoundrels undoubtedly deserve the severest punishment, but only they can possibly save the Lady Zamarind now."

"Then so be it!" Lord Robat stood and pointed a trembling finger at Tym. "You shall go free. Cure my granddaughter and you shall have half my kingdom!"

The Runemaster coughed. "Actually, my Lord, thou dost not rule a Kingdom."

"Don't I?"

"No, my Lord. In any case, strictly speaking, thou art a democratically elected head of state with limited powers..."

"All right, all right. Then the man who cures my granddaughter shall have ten florins and a jolly good lunch!" Lord Robat pointed at Tym. "Fail, and your fate will be more terrible and cruel than you can possibly imagine."

"I dunno about that," Colyn whispered to Tym apprehensively. "I got a pretty vivid imagination." He shuddered.

The Runemaster nodded agreement and turned to Humfrey. "Is Captain Gorge without?"

The boggart raised an eyebrow. "Without what? Oh, you mean outside. Sure, I got the old phoney on ice."

"Then send him in." The Runemaster looked pleased with himself. "The Runes foresaw that we would be needing him."

A bellowing from the passage heralded the arrival of Captain Gorge, who was frogmarched in by two guards and forced to kneel before Lord Robat. Luigi trotted in on their heels and bowed to the Runemaster. "He was jus' where you said he'd be, boss: hidin' in one o' my wine barrels."

Humfrey grinned. "A wine barrel? Wash it empty?"

"Not when 'e hid in it." Luigi gave Captain Gorge a filthy look.

"Traitor!" howled the captain. "After all the rot-gut grog I've supped at your bumboat of a tavern…"

"Oh, shut your'a head!" Luigi told him crossly. "You only come inna my restaurant to spy ona my customers – an' you never pay me for all the wine you drink anyways."

"Careen me on a lee shore and rove me with barnacles," roared Captain Gorge and belched. "Is this any way to treat a harmless old seafarin' man…?" His complaints tailed off as one of the guards put a sword to his throat.

"Why have you brought this creature here?" Lord Robat growled at the Runemaster.

"Because, my Lord, the Runes say – and I find this difficult to believe, but the Runes never lie – the Runes say that this rascal, this scapegrace, this good-for-nothing, blackguardly ruffian…"

"Steady as she goes, shipmate!" protested Captain Gorge.

"…can lead us to the Cumhera," concluded the Runemaster.

"The Cumhera! Why didn't you say so?" Captain Gorge gave Lord Robat a sly look. "Sure, I could help you find the Cumhera… but what's in it for poor old Captain Gorge?"

"Your life," said Lord Robat icily, "and if you are co-operative and very, very fortunate, the bits of your body I plan to confiscate before ending it."

"Spoken like an officer an' a gennleman!" Captain Gorge licked his lips nervously. "What was yer wantin' to know, maties?"

"Where and how you saw the Cumhera."

"You' a'wastin' your time," sneered Luigi. "This overstuffed wineskin, he's no more a sea-captain than I am."

"Mutiny, blast my beam ends," roared the captain. "By thunder—"

"Ah, pipe'a down, you old fraud."

The Runemaster gave the Pastafarian a twisted smile. "Thou art mistaken, my friend – at least in part."

"Oh, you gotta be pullin' my lasagna!" Luigi looked disgusted. "Are you tell me tha' ol' vermicelli whiskers 'ere really is a sailor?"

"Yes, though not a captain." The Runemaster turned to Captain Gorge who was now looking uncomfortable. "I believe the highest rank thou reached was – cabin boy?"

"'Tis a foul lie!" howled the captain. "Becalm and belay me—"

"Yes, yes, we know all that," said the Runemaster. "But I also know that thou came from a city far away, and when thou wast a boy, thou ran away to sea. Thou wast a sailor for three years, in the crew of the notorious Pirate Captain Grogbreath – until thou wast caught canoodling with thy captain's daughter."

Captain Gorge's bloodshot eyes filled with tears. "My little Leysa; a fine, spirited wench. She could shoot a cork out of a bottle at a hundred paces, fight off a shark with a blunt penknife, an' spit into the teeth of a hurricane to hit a revenue man in the eye, bless her. The love of me life, shipmates."

"Be that as it may," said the Runemaster drily, "Captain Grogbreath disapproved of thee and turned thee ashore. Many weary miles thou walked through the Forest, over many years – until in the end, thou reached Dun Indewood. Is that not so?"

"I tell ee, I were a captain!" Gorge insisted petulantly. The Runemaster shook his head.

"Would you believe lieutenant?" The Runemaster raised an eyebrow.

"Well, would you believe midshipman?" The Runemaster raised the other eyebrow. "Bo'sun? Able seaman? Ordinary seaman? Ship's cook?"

"Cabin boy," said the Runemaster emphatically.

"All right, all right!" snarled Gorge. "Take away an old sailorman's character…"

"Nevertheless," continued the Runemaster, "our friend here has seen much, as the Runes have revealed to me. His ship was swept far across the sea in a terrible storm, and on a far shore he and his shipmates found a fabulous treasure guarded by the Cumhera. Many of the crew fell victim to the creature's fiery breath. In spite of this, the young cabin boy planned to return one day and claim the treasure for his own. To that end, he drew a map.

"On their return, the pirates marooned young boy Gorge on a sandbank at the mouth of the Forest River. Then they sailed away, only to be wrecked shortly afterwards on a rocky shore, where most of the company perished – including the dreaded Captain Grogbreath himself."

"Aye," muttered Gorge sentimentally. "And what became of me dear, sweet little Leysa, no man could tell." He blew his nose moistly into an indescribable handkerchief.

The Runemaster gave Gorge a disapproving look. "Have you anything to add to my account?" he asked.

"Them Runes o' yourn be right tattle-tales, b'aint they, Admiral?" said Gorge sourly. He stuck his beard out defiantly. "Well, suppose there was a map – which I ain't sayin' there is, mind – if there was a map, an' your Runes knows everythin', where be this map now? Tell me that!"

Calmly, the Runemaster said, "It's hidden in your peg-arm."

"Now that ain't fair!" Gorge stamped his feet and swore horribly. "Spyin' on an old sailorman, a'peepin' and a'prying…"

"I leave that sort of thing to you." The Runemaster held out his hand. "Give me the map!"

"Over my dead body!"

Lord Robat said, "Certainly, if you insist."

Two guards stepped forward, unsheathing their swords. The fight went out of Captain Gorge. Muttering under his breath, he unscrewed his peg arm. From inside it, he drew a roll of parchment, cracked and yellow with age.

The Runemaster examined it. "How far away is this place?"

"Well may you ask, matey. Flog my pendants, 'tis a great and perilous journey – further than any landlubber from this 'ere City has ever been... further than the sky... further than thought... further than imagination..."

The Runemaster gave him a stare that a cockatrice would have been proud of. "And how far is that?"

Captain Gorge wilted. "A thousand miles, give or take a cable."

"Very well." The Runemaster turned to Tym and Colyn. "The Lady Zamarind will not survive more than a few days. Find the Cumhera, take its scale and return in time to save the Lady Zamarind, and thou art free. If she dies before thy return, thou wilt have cause to regret that they mother ever bore thee." The Runemaster stared hard at Tym. "Humfrey will again release the wish hounds to follow thee. He will instruct them, if at any time thou showest the slightest inclination to relinquish thy quest, to tear thee to pieces. But my friend the boggart is right. A Whizzard caused this mischief – only a Whizzard can undo it."

CHAPTER FIFTEEN

Ⱨow Tym and Colyn Slowed Down to Speed Up and met a number of Curious Beasts.

Tym and Colyn stood under the eaves of the Dark Forest. They were carrying sleeping rolls, hunting knives and packs containing water and provisions for several days.

"You won'ta need any more," Luigi had told them with a sympathetic grimace, "'cos if you ain't back before you finish your rations, you won't be able to eat anyway on account o' bein' dead."

Tym shucked his pack into a more comfortable position and stared into the Forest. Beneath the trees, the sunlight faltered and faded into a dappled twilight of gloom and vague shadows. He looked back. Behind stood the Runemaster,

Humfrey and Luigi along with a dozen or so men-at-arms, some of whom patted their crossbows in a meaningful sort of way. At a level with Tym's thigh, an invisible wish hound growled softly. Tym shrugged, and stepped into the shade of the trees.

Instantly, he was in a different world – different even from the open clearings and wide pathways of his own village, far different from the warmth and bustle of Dun Indewood.

The trees crowded around Tym and Colyn, silent but watchful. Briars and brambles lay in wait to trip the unwary. There were rustlings in the bushes on either side of the path. Further away, leaves shook as if disturbed by some prowling, unseen menace. Tym tried to stop his hands shaking.

The Forest was old. On its ancient trees the bark was wrinkled and scabby. Gnarled and twisted branches swayed slowly in the breeze. They seemed to be reaching towards him, their twigs twitching like stealthy fingers…

"Spoooky," whispered Colyn.

Tym jumped and spun round. "Don't creep up on me like that!" He glared at Colyn. "What's the matter with you? I thought you were used to being in the Forest."

"Well, yeah…" The small thief's voice was unsteady and his chin wobbled a bit. "But then I'm always wiv me dad, or Big Jim, or some o' the lads, an' now it's just you an' me…"

Tym sighed. "Don't worry. Just keep your mind on the job. Just say to yourself, nothing's going to go wrong…"

"Well, helllooooo there!"

Tym stopped dead at the familiar voice and groaned. "Not you again!"

The Highwaywolf grinned toothily. "Yes, me again. Awfully glad you could come. Pleased to… ha ha… *eat* you." The wolf crouched, ready to spring, its teeth bared in a snarl… and hesitated. His victims weren't cowering as expected.

Tym said to Colyn, "He's going to eat us. Dearie me!"

Colyn said to Tym, "Perhaps we should be goin'."

Tym said to Colyn, "I think you're right. On the count of three?"

They said together, "One… two… three…"…And vanished.

The wolf stared in astonishment. "Where'd they go? Where'd they go?"

Then it heard a sound. Several loud, growly sounds such as might be made by a pack of invisible hounds who would all put "giving a wolf something to remember us by" right at the top of their wish list.

The wolf gulped. "Oh, my stars…" it said faintly.

The wish hounds got their wish.

"'Ow long we been walkin'?" asked Colyn quite a lot later.

"Why?"

"'Cos I'm 'ungry."

"Then we may as well eat." Tym shrugged off his pack and sat down on a small patch of wiry grass. Around him, several patches of grass flattened as some of the wish hounds lay down. The sound of their panting was loud in the still air of the Forest.

Colyn looked up at the sky, what little of it could be seen through the thick foliage of the Forest canopy. "Yeah, but it isn't noon yet – I mean, the sun's not high enough..."

"No, it wouldn't be." Tym took a small loaf of bread out of his pack. "We're moving at Whizzard speed, remember. In normal time, we've only just come into the Forest – a few minutes ago at most. Humfrey and the guards won't be halfway back to the City yet."

"But we've walked miles!"

"I know." Tym eyed the loaf ruefully. "I've been thinking things out. Luigi was wrong. Moving at Whizzard speed, we can cover hundreds of miles in a few days of normal time. But that doesn't make the journey any shorter for us. We'll still have to walk those miles and in Whizzard time that'll take... well, ages."

Colyn sat down all of a heap. "I fink I lost you after you said, 'Luigi was wrong'."

"When we're moving at Whizzard speed, everyone around us looks as if they're not moving at all: but they are really, it's just that we're moving so much faster that they look to us as if they're standing still."

"Yeah..."

"It seems to us that we've been walking for a long time, but in the normal world, hardly any time has passed. We'll be tired soon. We'll have been walking for what seems like hours and hours, and if we were moving in normal time it'd be getting dark and time for bed. But we're not operating in normal time. As far as the rest of the world is concerned, it will still be early in the morning."

"Yeah, I see that…"

"We can't wait until it gets dark to go to sleep, because that won't happen for ages in our time. A day in the normal world will last a long time for us! We might have to go to sleep and get up again – oh, I don't know – maybe a hundred times before it gets dark in the normal world."

"Strewf!"

"Yes. But the distance we have to travel hasn't changed just because we're moving at Whizzard speed."

"So we could be walkin' for munfs an' munfs in Whizzard time…"

"…and only be gone for a few days in normal time. That's right. In fact it's our only hope – because we can walk a hundred miles in the time it would take somebody walking at normal speed to go to the privy and back! Otherwise we wouldn't stand a chance of reaching the Cumhera and getting back in time to save the Lady Zamarind."

"But all that time will still pass for us, right?" Colyn looked horrified. "I mean, our bodies will get older at the speed we're livin' at, which is Whizzard speed. So if we're travellin' for ages at Whizzard speed we'll be ages older by the time we get back, but people livin' at normal speed will only have aged a few days!"

"That's right," nodded Tym.

Colyn gave a low whistle. "It's like them stories you 'ear about people bein' took off by the fairies, an' they only spend a night wiv 'em, but then the fairies give them a horse to ride 'ome, an' it's all different, an' they ask somebody if they've ever 'eard of them, an' they say, 'Wossisname? Oh, 'e disappeared a 'undred years ago.' An' they get off the 'orse an' the minute they touch the ground they crumble into dust…"

"We won't be gone long enough for that to happen." Tym threw the last crust of his bread towards the wish hounds: phantom teeth snatched at it in mid-air and it vanished. Tym brushed his hands. "Aren't you going to eat anything?"

Colyn shook his head. "Suddenly, I'm not 'ungry." He sighed gustily. "So we just got to keep walkin' an' walkin' an' walkin', never seein' annuver livin' fing (leastways, not one that's movin'), until we reach the Cumhera's country. That's gonna be dead borin' that is."

"You're right," said Tym. At that moment, inspiration struck him. "Unless…"

"Unless what?"

"Think about it." Tym could hardly speak for excitement. Fighting to keep his voice level, he went on, "Look, so far we've only been able to go at two speeds, haven't we? Whizzard speed and everyday speed."

"Well, yeah," agreed Colyn, "but…"

"What if there are in-between speeds? We don't know that there aren't, we just haven't tried to find them. Suppose we could run faster than the wind, but not so fast that everything around us seems to stop moving?"

Colyn said slowly, "Then we could still do the job in a few days of our time, as well as a few days of normal time." He gave Tym a huge grin. Then his face fell and he shook his head. "But we don't even know wevver we can do it…"

"Then let's find out." Tym scrambled to his feet and hurriedly donned his pack. "Ready?"

Looking into each other's eyes, Tym and Colyn chorused: "Fast… faster… go!"

In a blur of movement, they were off. The surprised wish hounds looked at each other with their phantom eyes and their phantom mouths broke into big, doggy grins. A run! This was more like it! The Forest echoed to a wild chorus of howls as the pack streamed in pursuit.

Tym's mind was buzzing. His heart was pounding from sheer joy. To think he had never realised that a Whizzard could do this! It was wonderful. The running was effortless. Although he was going so fast that the trees of the Forest were little more than a green-and-brown blur, he wasn't out of breath. He felt he could keep this up for ever! Nimbly, he sidestepped a larch and pounded on, exulting in the sensation of speed. It wasn't really like running at all – it was more like falling sideways, from a cliff so high that he would never reach the bottom…

Colyn raced alongside him. "Hey, Tym!" he yelled. "Can't catch me!" He put his head down and shot ahead. With a whoop, Tym followed.

In a clearing in the Dark Forest, a family of bears was sitting on a hollow log. The female bear was scolding the male bear, who had a hangdog expression on his face. "'Let's go for a walk while our porridge cools down…' What a great idea that was. And what is Junior going to eat now, if I may be so bold as to inquire?"

The youngest bear snuffled.

"And what's he going to sit on, for that matter, Mr Cheapskate? Or sleep in? I wanted to get that nice, sturdy little bed but oh, no." Putting on a high pitched voice, she mimicked, "'What's the point, he'll only outgrow it, let's get the cheaper bed, that'll do for now…' – and where's this cheaper bed, pray? In bits all over the floor, that's where!"

"Well, who'd have thought some great lump of a girl would go and lie in it?" grumbled the male bear defensively. "It wasn't designed for that. Goldilocks? More like Goldie-Bricks, if you ask me. Kids today – I blame the parents."

"At least you could've shifted your big furry butt and caught her."

"She was too fast," complained the bear. Instantly, he knew he'd made a mistake.

"*Too fast?*" screeched Mother Bear. "A human, too fast for a bear?"

There was a rushing sound, two streaks of blurred movement and suddenly two humans were standing before the surprised bears.

"Excuse me," said the taller human politely, "I think we might have lost our way a bit – could you tell me which way is North?"

Wordlessly, Father Bear pointed.

"Thanks very much." The two figures shot off between the trees. Saplings and branches bent with the speed of their passing. Leaves thrashed in their wake. A cloud of dust and leaf mould flew from their pounding feet and hung in the still air long after the rush of their passage. Silence. The bears looked at each other.

Then there was another rushing, with a galloping of great paws. The bears huddled together for protection until the baying of the pursuing pack of phantom hounds had died away in the distance.

Father Bear carefully unclasped Mother Bear's paws from round his neck. "Were you saying something about humans not being fast?" he said acidly, pointing the way Tym and Colyn, now long out of sight, had gone. He gave a disdainful sniff. "I rest my case."

Slower… slowest… "Whoooohooooo!" Laughing and gasping for breath, Tym and Colyn skidded to a halt, leaving four long grooves in the powdery earth of the Forest floor. With a rushing of paws and much panting, the wish hounds romped into the clearing behind them.

Colyn lay on his back and crowed in triumph. "That was great! I could go on for ever! Why did we stop?" He rolled over and grinned at Tym. "Come on, let's keep going…"

Tym grinned back, but shook his head. "Too dangerous. It's getting too dark to see properly. Did you ever stop to think what would happen if one of us ran into a tree at the speed we've been going?"

"No…"

"Think about it now."

Colyn did, and made a face. "Ooer. Messy."

"Exactly," nodded Tym. "So we stop here, make a fire and eat. Collect some wood." Tym took his tinderbox from his pack. Before long, he had made a blazing fire which cut through the darkness. Huddling close to its protective warmth, the two travellers tucked into their meagre rations.

Tym gave a yawn. "I don't know about you, but I'm tired."

"Yeah, me too." Colyn looked around. "Trouble is, now we're not moving at Whizzard speed, we're like, vulnerable. Know what I mean? There's all kinds of fings in the Forest that'd gobble us up for supper. We ought to set a watch."

"I suppose you're right," said Tym sleepily. Then he raised a hand and in more alert tones said, "Listen."

Colyn listened. "I can't 'ear nothin'."

"Neither can I. Where are the hounds?"

The little thief shrugged. "I 'eard 'em go off into the Forest. Probably chasin' phantom rabbits."

Just then, there was a rustling in the bushes around the clearing and an outburst of hysterical giggling. Tym leapt to his feet and seized a burning branch from the fire. "Who's there?"

The only response was insane shrieks of laughter. Tym gripped the branch tighter. "Who are you? What do you want?"

A voice from the darkness said, "'Ello, 'ello. No, listen, don't mess about. You look like a couple of blokes who like a good laugh. Have you heard the one about the travelling salestroll and the boggart's daughter?"

Chapter Sixteen

How Tym's rescuers Rose to the Occasion, showing that where there's a Will there's a Way.

Tym stared at the creature that emerged cautiously from the bushes and paced around the clearing at the edge of the firelight.

"There was this salestroll, see – stop me if you've heard it, – and he gets lost, see…"

The creature looked something like a dog, but its back legs were shorter than its front ones and it carried its tail tucked down between them, giving it the peculiar gait of a dog that's just been given a kick up the backside. Its coat, which looked as if it had been preserved by a particularly ham-fisted taxidermist, was part-striped and part-spotted. Its lips were drawn back over its teeth in a manic grin and its grating voice continued relentlessly, "So it's almost daylight, see, so he sees this boggart's house, right. So he knocks on the door, right, and the boggart comes to the door, and he says – the troll, not the boggart – he says, 'Have you got a cave for the light?'"

Tym had never heard of laughing hyenas. If he had, he would have known better than to go on listening. He would have known that these odd, unfinished looking creatures were among the most feared predators in the Forest.

"...And the boggart says, yeah, all right, but you'll have to share a room with the gremlin, right, so he does, and..."

The hyenas had a terribly cunning and cruel way of making their prey helpless. They would gang up on travellers and tell them really long and absolutely awful jokes until they bored them to death. Then they would pounce and rip their victims to pieces.

"So the gremlin says, 'Is that what it was? Blimey, I thought I was being attacked by a rockery!'" The hyena rolled around on the ground, screaming with laughter. Tym felt his eyelids droop. Colyn was swaying on his feet.

Another hyena prowled forward, its lips drawn back in a dreadful grin. "Here, I got a good one. You'll like this. So anyway, right, there was a ghoul, a leprechaun and a banshee, right, and they're sitting in this tavern, right..."

Tym felt a terrible numbness spreading over him. The joke went on and on and on. The hyenas' inane grins, mindless cheeriness and shrill, monotonous voices were working their dreadful spell on a mind and body already wearied by long travel.

"…And the leprechaun says, 'Beggorah, I've got it! The brown pixie's bigger than the orange one!'" Once again the hyenas screamed with mirth and circled closer. Colyn's eyes were glazing over.

"Here's a good one! What's the difference between a bogie and a boggart? You don't get boggarts up your nose!"

"What do you get if you mix a dragon and a mouse? Something that burns very big holes in the skirting board!"

"What's a gnome's favourite song? *Gnome, gnome on the range*…" The hyenas cackled insanely and licked their chops.

Tym slumped to the ground. "Can't take any more," he muttered through clenched teeth. Desperately, he tried to force himself to rise, but it was no good: he seemed simply to have lost the will to live. The hyenas edged closer, ready for the kill…

Tym had given himself up for lost when, as though from far away and through impenetrable mists of oblivion, he heard a rushing of paws and a deep baying. The hyenas stopped and pricked up their ears nervously. Moments later, they screamed with terror and fled blindly in all directions as the wish hounds bounded back into the clearing. Tym and Colyn shook off their deadly lethargy as their tormentors fled, yelping in agony as phantom teeth snapped at their heels.

To his amazement, Tym heard a voice ring through the Forest. "Go on! Chase them! Bite them! See them off; good boys."

A moment later, the owner of the voice leapt over a bush into the clearing. It was a girl, of about Tym's age, slim and dark-haired. She was carrying a crossbow. She brought this up sharply and pointed it at a hyena who, braver or luckier than its fellows, had succeeded in evading the wish hounds and was stalking towards her, snarling.

"What do you call a man who strokes a hyena on the head?" she asked in a friendly voice.

The hyena wasn't in the mood for jokes now, but it had to respond. "I don't know," it answered sullenly.

"Pat. What do you call a hyena with two legs shorter than the others?"

"I don't know."

"Eileen. What do you call a hyena with an arrow sticking out from its backside?"

The hyena snarled, "I don't know!"

"What's your name?"

"Roofus."

"You call it Roofus."

The hyena thought about this. "That's not funny."

"You'd better believe it." The girl took aim.

With a snarl, the hyena turned and fled. The girl fired, the arrow speeding to its target. The hyena yelped and shot into the cover of the Forest.

"Told you," said the girl smugly.

The three remaining hyenas saw that the crossbow had been fired and leapt. Suddenly, there was a boy beside the girl. He was wearing a battered breastplate and holding a sword, which flashed in the light of the fire as he brought the flat of the blade down across the hyenas' flanks with stinging force. Yelping, they retreated and finally the clearing was empty of their ghastly snarls and cackles.

The girl turned to the boy. "What kept you?" she asked calmly.

"There were more gathering in the trees: I had to chase them off first," said the boy. He sheathed his sword and unslung an odd triangular-shaped bag from his back.

A grating voice rose in complaint from the folds of the pack. "When you've finished playing games with those fleabitten mutts, would it be too much trouble to let me out of here, Mr Hero?"

The boy grinned and drew from the bag a beautifully crafted harp. Its frame was topped with a carved wooden head wearing a crown and an expression of sullen discontent.

The boy bowed. "May I present the Harp of the Kings," he said formally. After a moment, he gave the Harp a sharp nudge. "Say hello."

The Harp scowled at Tym and Colyn. "Charmed, I'm sure," it said sourly. "Don't bother to thank us. Oh, you didn't. Must you go so soon? Don't let us keep you."

Tym and Colyn stared at their rescuers in speechless amazement.

The boy gave them an amiable smile and held out a hand. "Hello," he said brightly. "My name's Will. This is Rose. Have you come far?"

They all gathered round the fire. At a word from Rose, the wish hounds spread out and formed a picket line around the camp, to guard against any further attack.

"Your hounds must have heard me out in the Forest," said Rose. "Or smelt me, maybe."

"Probably smelt you," said the Harp snidely. "How long is it since you took a bath?"

Rose ignored this. "Anyway, the hounds came over to say hello – we're old friends."

Colyn coughed as some of the herbal tea Rose had brewed went down the wrong way. "Friends?" he croaked in disbelieving tones.

"Yes. We used to go hunting pheasants."

"Pheasants?"

"Well, phantom pheasants."

Colyn stared. "Are there many phantom pheasants in the Forest?"

The Harp cackled. "None at all."

Colyn shook his head in bewilderment. Rose gave him a sidelong look. "Did you ever go fishing in the Trickle?"

"Yeah – 'course."

"Ever catch anything?"

Colyn shook his head. "Don't be stoopid, there ain't no fish in the Trickle."

"There you are then." Rose sat back with the self-satisfied expression of someone who has produced an unanswerable argument.

The Harp thrummed disgustedly to itself. "Humans. Crazy or what?"

Tym took a small loaf of bread from his pack: he thought for a moment, then broke it in two and passed half to Will, who accepted the stale offering courteously. Tym nudged Colyn, who started, and then took a loaf from his own pack to share with Rose.

"I've heard of you," Tym said to Will. "You saved the City from Lord Gordin."

"With a little help from his friends," said Rose demurely.

"Yeah, such as a brave and unsung Harp whose selfless devotion and unfailing cheerfulness have gone shamefully unrecognised—" The Harp gave a squeak as Rose grabbed it by its wooden throat.

"You can be quiet," she told it, "or you can be firewood. Choose." The Harp shut up, muttering darkly.

"So what are you doing out here in the Forest?" Tym asked their newfound friends.

Will shrugged. "Travelling. Exploring. Seeing what's out here."

"And what have you found?"

Will gave Tym a considering look. "Well, just at the moment, we seem to have found you two. What are *you* doing here?"

Tym hesitated. Should he tell the truth? Then he shrugged; there was no good reason not to. In any case, Will seemed pretty shrewd – he'd probably see right through any deception, and Rose would certainly resent it. Giving Rose cause for resentment was clearly not a good idea. "Well," he said carefully, "it happened like this..."

Will listened gravely as Tym explained their quest, with frequent interruptions from Colyn and occasional wry comments from Rose. When he'd finished, the Harp gave a bark of laughter. "Boy o boy," it sneered. "Did you stiffs foul up good!" Its strings jangled, and it sang a sarcastic little song:

> *"Half a jar of essence of Air,*
> *Add some Earth and Water;*
> *Boil the mix and swig it down,*
> *Though you didn't oughter!*
> *Aggravate a cockatrice,*
> *Stun the High Lord's daughter!*
> *Then into the Forest like*
> *Lambs to the slaughter!"*

The Harp cackled.

"She's Lord Robat's granddaughter," said Tym sullenly, "not his daughter."

"I knew that!" snarled the Harp. "'Granddaughter' doesn't fit, so I used a little poetic licence, is that all right with you? Suddenly, everyone's a critic!"

Will sat staring into the fire for a while. Then he said, "If Humfrey and the Runemaster hadn't sent you into the Forest to find the Cumhera's scale, would you have come anyway?"

Tym thought for a moment. "Yes," he said slowly. "Yes, I would."

Will gazed steadily at Tym. "And would you keep on until you found it, no matter what? Even if Humfrey hadn't set the wish hounds after you?" There was an outburst of panting as the phantom dogs pricked up their ears. Rose made shushing noises and they settled down again.

Tym nodded. "You probably don't think much of me…"

"Oh, I don't know," the Harp broke in. "For a thief, a faker, a liar and a murderer you seem like a reasonably nice guy… *ow*!" The Harp glared at Rose, who had flung a fallen crab apple at it. "Willya mind the varnish? Sheesh!"

"I remember something Zamarind said," Tym went on. "She said she had to guard the Firestones, even if it cost her her life, because she'd made a promise." Tym shrugged. "She said it was an aristocracy thing."

Will looked thoughtful. "I think she was wrong about that," he said carefully. "Rich people like to think they deserve to be rich because they're more honourable than anybody else—"

"Sure!" the Harp chimed in. "That way when they're robbing somebody blind or making someone else's life a misery for their own gain, they can say, 'Hey, this can't really be wrong because I'm doing it and I have a sense of honour'!"

Will continued, "Zamarind was brought up in a palace and she knows only what she's been told by others of noble birth. But the truth is that anybody can act honourably – if they choose to." Tym nodded slowly.

"Honour can be a burden," said Will. "You can't use it as a weapon. You can't spend it. It may cost you dear." He picked up a stick and poked at the fire. "It's only worth is the value you place upon it in yourself – and in others. It is hard to come by and easily lost."

Tym, for no reason he could name, felt sulky and cross. "Then what use is it?" he demanded pettishly. Will said nothing, but Rose gave Tym an unusually sympathetic look.

"Just this," she said. "If you act honourably, you will always know what you should do: and even though doing it may cause you pain or loss, you will always be true to your true self."

Tym sat bolt upright. The Dreamwalker had used those exact words, the first time they had met. *"Only be true to your true self and you will gain your heart's desire."* But Tym had taken it to mean, 'Keep trying to be a wizard and one day you will be a wizard', and that wasn't what the Dreamwalker had meant at all. He'd meant, 'Do what you know to be right and you will always be at peace with yourself.'

Tym stood up abruptly and walked unsteadily off into the trees. Rose raised an eyebrow. Will shook his head.

The Harp called out, "Yah! Cry-baby! Look at the big—" but its snide remarks were muffled by Rose, who promptly popped the carrying bag over its head.

Later that night, Colyn woke up. Will was asleep and Rose was sitting by the fire, on guard. A fallen tree lay on one side of the clearing. Tym was sitting there alone on the dead trunk, legs crossed and shoulders bowed, silhouetted against the silvery light of the rising moon.

Tym joined the others for a meagre breakfast, saying nothing. When they had struck camp, he turned to Will and Rose. "We'd better be getting on," he said.

Will nodded. "We'd offer to help, but if you can move as fast as you say you can, we'd only hold you back." He grinned suddenly and held out his hand. Tym, startled, hesitated for a moment, then he smiled shyly and shook it.

"Do you need the wish hounds?" asked Will casually. "They can come with us if you'd rather."

Rose gave him a sharp look. "Will, Humfrey sent—" Will cleared his throat and Rose fell silent.

"Hey," complained the Harp, "don't I get any say in this? Who wants a pack of pesky phantom pooches rampaging about? I warn you, if you leave me on the ground, and one of them even thinks about cocking its phantom leg—" Rose clapped a hand over its strings, which hummed like a hive of angry bees.

Tym said, slowly, "I daresay we can get along without them."

"'Course," chipped in Colyn, "they're worth a fair bit, rare pack of valuable, fully trained phantom 'ounds..." Tym elbowed him in the ribs. "Our gift to you," continued Colyn seamlessly. "No payment necessary. Wouldn't dream of it."

Will nodded briskly and turned to Rose. "Call them, and we'll be off."

Rose frowned. "Will..." Will raised an eyebrow. "All right, all right!" Rose put her fingers to her lips and gave a shrill whistle. Immediately, the clearing was full of the commotion of the phantom pack as they milled around Rose who bent double, apparently explaining what they were to do. There were a couple of questioning whines, but when Tym and Colyn set off across the clearing, the hounds stayed behind.

"Well, no sense hangin' about," said Colyn after a few yards. "Ready?"

Tym squared his shoulders and nodded. "Ready." The Whizzard and his companion took off.

Rose stared at the space where they'd been. She blinked dust out of her eyes and picked twigs out of her hair. "Impressive."

Will nodded. Rose gave him a hard stare. "Are you sure you did the right thing? After all, Humfrey sent the wish hounds to make sure Tym completes his quest."

"People change. I did. I don't think Tym needs the hounds to make him keep his promise." Will shrugged. "Time will tell."

"I hate you when you're being masterful." With an unladylike snort, Rose set off into the Forest. Will grinned, slung the Harp over his back and followed.

For the rest of that day, Tym and Colyn made uninterrupted progress. Tym thought of their running speed as 'Faster-Than-The-Wind-Speed'. Then he decided this was a bit cumbersome and thought of it simply as 'Wind Speed'. He and Colyn drank from Forest streams, and at noon they slowed their pace to look for food. Colyn spotted a cluster of fruit trees a little way to one side of their path. The apples and pears were some way past their best, but they ate several and stuffed a few more inside their packs for later.

As the sun began to set, they reached an area of open grassland. In the dying light, Tym pored over Captain Gorge's map. "If this is accurate," he said, "we're nearing the country of the Cumhera. We've crossed these six streams, going to the North-east…" His forefinger traced their route. "Once we're across this range of hills here… we should be nearly at the coast. Then we have to find some way to cross the sea." He folded the map and brooded. "I hope we make it in time."

Colyn nodded. "Before the Lady Zamarind turns 'er toes up, yer mean."

Tym was too preoccupied to protest about Colyn's choice of words. "Yes, that: but there's something else, too."

"Wot?"

"Remember how the potion wore off just when I was trying to prove to your dad that I really was a Whizzard?"

"Yeah."

"Well, that was only a few days after I took it. I have no idea how much longer this dose will last."

Colyn's face fell. "Ooer. We don't want to be stuck out 'ere in the Forest wiv no potion to get us 'ome."

Tym gave him a stern look. "And no way of helping the Lady Zamarind."

"Oh, yeah, that goes wivout sayin'," said Colyn hurriedly. He thought for a moment. "Maybe when we're not movin' at full Whizzard speed, we don't use it up so fast."

"Maybe. Who knows?" Tym shook his head worriedly. "Anyway, the grassland seems to go right to the hills. We can save time if we cross it tonight. There aren't any trees, so we shan't run into anything."

Colyn nodded. "Let's go."

They set off with the last rays of the sun disappearing to their left. They were both moving at a steady run when, without warning, the ground collapsed beneath them. It was like falling into quicksand. At wind speed, the collapse happened so slowly that Colyn and Tym sank through the disintegrating Forest floor like flies drowning in syrup. With despairing cries, the Whizzard and his companion were drawn into a slow-motion maelstrom of rock and dust, and disappeared.

CHAPTER SEVENTEEN

How Tym and Colyn dropped in for Dinner and found that Gobblings have Gnome Manners.

When Tym came to, he was lying face down, covered in debris. Wincing with pain – his body seemed to be one huge bruise – he shook the heaviest of the fallen rocks off his back and slowly sat up. Wherever he was, it was pitch dark. "Colyn!" he called. "Colyn!"

There was a moan from somewhere to his right. Feeling his way carefully, Tym found a foot sticking out from a pile of rubble. He began to clear rocks away. Eventually, with a clatter of dislodged stones, Colyn sat up. "Ooooh, my 'ead…" Then his voice rose in panic. "Tym… Tym! I can't see!"

"Neither can I. There's no light down here."

"Oh, fank goodness. I thought I'd gone blind." Colyn groaned. "Where are we?"

Tym shrugged – a waste of time, as Colyn couldn't possibly see him. "No idea," he said.

After a long silence, Colyn said, "Ah, well, I suppose we'd better try an' find a way out. I don't suppose nothin' is goin' to come an' rescue us, down here."

From the surrounding darkness, a low and very gloomy voice said, "Gnot bloomin' likely!"

There was a longer and much more worried silence. Then, in a quavering voice, Tym called out, "Who's there?"

There was a muttering from the darkness. Then another voice said, "Gnot telling!"

Tym tried again. "We mean you no harm! Will you help us?"

"Gno."

"I mean, will you tell us the way out of here?"

"Gno."

"Then leave us alone and go on your way."

"Gno."

"I know what they are!" said Colyn suddenly. "They're gnomes." There was unhappy muttering from the darkness all about them. "Aren't yer?" demanded Colyn.

"Gno," said a voice, but without conviction.

"Yes, yer are." Colyn lowered his voice and told Tym, "There's a few of 'em come to live in the City. Big Jim knows 'em. They're sorta brownies, like 'im, only they live underground."

"Gno we bloomin' don't," muttered the voice in sullen tones.

"Where are we now, then?" demanded Colyn. There was

no reply. "Trouble wiv gnomes is," he went on confidentially, "they contradict everythin' yer say."

"We gnever!"

"See what I mean?" Colyn gave an angry snort.

"Well, don't antagonise them," whispered Tym urgently. "We need their help. They can obviously see down here…"

"Gno we bloomin' can't!"

"…so they can help us to get out."

There was a chorus of angry mutters. "Gnothing doing!" snarled the spokesgnome.

"Why not?" demanded Tym, exasperated. "What have we done to you?"

"Humans is gnasty," said another voice. There was a chorus of agreement.

"They give us bloomin' silly gnames," agreed a third voice. "'Knockers', 'Coblynau', 'Kobbolds'. Gets on your bloomin' gnerves."

"Then they come down here," grumbled the first voice, "living fifty of them to a bloomin' mine, taking our jobs, stealing our women."

Tym's imagination boggled. "Stealing your women?"

"Yeah!" said the voice belligerently. "We've seen the size of their bloomin' mattocks. Turn a young girl's head, bloomin' mattocks that size."

Tym tried again. "Look, we're not miners and we don't want to stay here. We haven't even got any mattocks!"

There was a chorus of sniggers, then the sound of footsteps and a sharp exclamation. A commanding voice said, "What's going on here?"

A light flared up in the darkness. Tym and Colyn blinked, trying to shield their eyes with their hands. When they could see again, they realised that they were in a fair-sized cavern. They were surrounded by little men who did, indeed, look rather like Big Jim except that they were dressed in knee britches, collarless shirts and leather waistcoats. Each of the gnomes was carrying a businesslike pick with a sharpened blade on the other side, and they were all wearing clogs, brightly coloured, patterned headscarves and disgruntled expressions.

In their midst, and staring curiously at Tym and Colyn, was a youngish-looking gnome dressed more richly than the rest. His headscarf had gold lace round the edge and his waistcoat was trimmed with fur. He wore a cloak and was holding a lantern above his head. "What have we here?" he said again.

A gnome with a particularly malevolent expression knuckled his forehead, and said, "Spies, Your Lowness."

"We ain't!" said Colyn crossly. "We've tried tellin' them, but they just disagree wiv every word we say."

The malevolent gnome scowled. "Do gnot."

"Do too!"

"Do gnot!"

"Do—"

"Enough!" The gnome with the lantern handed it to one of his followers and stepped forward, hand outstretched. "I'm most frightfully sorry. Do please forgive my men. They're not used to strangers."

Tym gaped for a moment, then took the proffered hand

and shook it warmly. "Don't mention it," he said politely.

The gnome grimaced. "Where are my manners? Feobold, Uncrowned Prince of the Gnomes, at your service."

Tym looked puzzled. "Uncrowned Prince?"

"Ah, yes," said Feobold breezily. "Among gnomes, royal protocol is a bit complicated. I can only be Crown Prince when I come of age. As a matter of fact, that's about to happen and I'm on my way to our capital city, Gnomansland, to be crowned." He waved a hand airily. "These chaps are my escort." The other gnomes bowed and knuckled their foreheads to Uncrowned Prince Feobold, who lowered his voice and went on in a confiding whisper, "Capital fellows of course, but a bit rough and ready, if you know what I mean."

He straightened up. "Well, enough about me. Would you mind most awfully telling me what you two are doing here? I mean, you're very welcome and all that..." There was a suppressed muttering of dissent from the other gnomes which Feobald pretended not to hear. "But this is my Kingdom, don't you know and all that; one likes to know what's going on."

Tym gave the Uncrowned Prince a condensed explanation of their presence. He didn't, for instance, mention the Lady Zamarind. He had an idea that the Prince wouldn't take kindly to people who stunned members of their own Royal Family with cockatrices.

"So we were making our way to the sea," he concluded, "and the ground suddenly gave way underneath us, and that's how we ended up down here."

Feobold held up his lantern, but the roof of the cavern was

beyond the reach of its beams. The hole Tym and Colyn had fallen through must have sealed tight behind them by rocks dislodged in their fall.

"So you see, we never meant to come here at all... I don't suppose," said Tym hopefully, "you could help us get back up there?"

"Gno." Feobold stopped abruptly and blushed. "I do beg your pardon. Force of habit. What I meant was, I don't think we can. This is one of our old airshafts. Since you weren't badly hurt when you fell, I suppose we can't be very far from the surface: but to get up there, we'd still need shoring and scaffolding and all kinds of stuff, and I'm afraid we really don't have time."

The angry-looking gnome stepped forward again, knuckling his forehead. "Just what I was going to say, Your Highness. Can't be too careful."

"All right, all right, Thugmug," said Feobold agreeably. "Point taken. No telling when the blighters might turn up, what?" He turned back to Tym and Colyn. "You'd better come with us."

Tym wasn't at all sure that this was a good idea. "Your Highness is most gracious..." he began.

Feobold waved a hand airily. "Oh, tush! Think nothing of it. If I can help somebody as I go along, and all that, as they used to say at the Old School..."

"The Old School, Your Highness?"

"Oh, yes, I went to the Knyght School in Dun Indewood. Do you know it?" Feobold became confidential again. "Under an assumed name, of course. I was only three hundred years old at the time: I could pass for a human boy at that age." He sighed. "Happy days!"

Tym tried to imagine the gnome Prince in the blue and red tabard of the Knyght School and failed dismally. He wondered how old Feobold was now, but decided it would be impolite to ask. "Well, if you're sure, Your Highness," he said. "We don't want to be any trouble…"

"Gno trouble at all!" said Feobold dismissively. "Much the best thing you could do. There's safety in gnumbers, after all." He turned on his heel and strode off down the cavern.

Tym hurried to keep up. "Safety from what?"

Feobold frowned. "Gobblings," he said shortly.

Tym turned to stare at Colyn, who was trotting along behind him; Colyn raised his eyebrows and shook his head. He had never heard of gobblings either. Tym turned back to Feobold and said, "Look, I don't want to seem stupid…"

Feobold stopped abruptly. "We don't like talking about gobblings," he said rather stiffly. "They're the traditional enemies of the gnomes, if you must know. Horrible, cunning, coarse, savage little brutes. Absolute rotters in fact. Gno manners. They undermine our tunnels, steal our treasure, attack us whenever they can. And they eat anything."

Colyn gave Tym an uneasy look. "Anyfink?"

"Oh, yes," said Feobold angrily. "Why d'you think they're called gobblings?" His face crumpled; he took out a lace handkerchief and dabbed at his eyes. "It was the gobblings that ate my poor, dear mother." All around him, the guard-gnomes sniffled and wiped their eyes surreptitiously.

"That's terrible!" exclaimed Tym.

Feobold blew his nose loudly. "Oh, well, it was a long time ago. All spoil down the shaft, as we say. But you can see why we don't like talking about gobblings." The Uncrowned Prince set off again. "Trouble is," he remarked over his shoulder, "Thugmug here thinks a band of them might be on our trail."

Thugmug nodded. "I've seen the signs," he said darkly.

Colyn cast a nervous glance behind him, and hurried into the middle of the escorting gnomes. "Still," he said with forced heartiness, "they won't attack us, right? I mean, there's lots of us an' we're well-armed..."

Feobold shook his head dubiously. "I wouldn't count on it. They're fierce little beggars and bumping off the Uncrowned Prince of their enemies would be a bit of a coup for them. And if they've been tracking us as long as old Thugmug thinks they have, they'll be getting pretty hungry by now."

Colyn gulped. "Hhhhungry?" Thugmug gave Colyn a wicked leer.

Tym had other things on his mind. "This city of yours," he said, "is it far? You see, our quest is urgent, and we—"

He broke off as the caverns were suddenly filled with nightmarish noises. Hoots, shrieks and howls echoed from all directions, along with a low pitched, rhythmic growl: "Gobblegobblegobblegobblegobblegobble..."

Thugmug gave a cry of rage and raised his mattock. "Gobblings!" The enemy was upon them.

The gobblings were shambling creatures about half the size of the gnomes: but what they lacked in size they more than made up for in viciousness. They seemed to be all hair, teeth and talons. Round their necks they wore small and very grubby napkins, and each carried an oversized knife and fork. There were hundreds of them. They swarmed over the defending gnomes. The cavern rang to the clash of mattock against cutlery.

Feobold had drawn his sword and was laying about him with gusto. As Tym watched, he sent a gobbling kinfe flying out of its owner's claw with a dextrous twist of his wrist. Tym caught a gobbling fork on his dagger and kicked its owner in the shins. Beside him, Colyn was wrestling a gobbling for its knife. Both humans had received a number of scratches and painful bites by the time Thugmug, his mattock notched in many places, fought his way to their side.

He saluted the Prince and panted, "Can't keep 'em off much longer."

Tym grabbed a gobbling that was leaping at Thugmug's throat and threw it over his shoulder. "What would happen to you if the Prince got away?"

Thugmug gave a mirthless guffaw. "Not much. They'd probably leave us alone. It's His Highness they want."

"All right. You've helped us – at least, you've tried to – so we'll help you." Tym avoided a vicious prod from a gobbling fork. "We'll get the Prince to safety. Just keep those creatures off for a few minutes."

Thugmug snorted. "You? Save the Prince? Gno chance!" Then he gave an angry shrug. "On the other hand, what have we got to lose?" The gnome raised his voice. "Come on, lads! Give them something to remember us by!" He charged back into the fray.

Tym turned to Colyn. "Ready?" Grim-faced, Colyn nodded. In an instant, they had shot to Whizzard speed. The scene in the cavern froze into immobility. It looked like a painting of Hades by an artist with a particularly unpleasant imagination.

Tym and Colyn hurried over to the Prince. "Sheave 'is sword," snapped Colyn. "We don't want that wavin' about – it'll 'ave our ears off!"

Tym secured the sword and picked up the lantern. Then, stumbling and groaning with effort, he and Colyn carried the motionless Prince away from the conflict and through a narrower passageway into another tunnel. Taking turns to carry the gnome, they staggered onwards.

Time passed. The tunnel narrowed. The going became harder. At length, they heard a muffled roaring ahead. Moving more cautiously, they arrived at a cleft in the rock. Here, they stopped and stared.

Before them, a stone bridge leapt in a single span across a deep gorge. In the bottom of the gorge, halted in its tempestuous flow, was a river. Waves paused in mid-swoosh as if made of ice, and spray hung in the air over the foaming water.

"Let's find out where we are." Tym set Prince Feobold down and locked gazes with Colyn. Slow... slower... slowest...

With a roar, the river thundered into life, crashing against the rock walls of the tunnel, filling it with stinging spume. The Prince looked around in astonishment. "Wha—? Where are we? Where are my men? Where are the gobblings?"

"Your Highness," said Tym urgently, "there's no time to explain. What is this place?"

Feobold was rubbing his head as though he suspected he'd been knocked unconscious. "Ah? Oh, this is the Gnomeden Gate Bridge. It's one of our ancient monuments: our city is just beyond. But—" He got no further.

"Gobblegobblegobblegobblegobblegobble…" Chanting their dreadul battle cry, a howling pack of gobblings came swarming down the tunnel towards them.

"Over the bridge, Your Highness!" Tym gave Feobold a push. "We'll hold them off."

Feobold opened his mouth to argue, then thought better of it. He saluted Tym and Colyn, then turned and made his way across the bridge to safety.

Before the Whizzard and his companion could speed up, the gobblings were upon them. The impetus of their charge and sheer weight of numbers shot Tym and Colyn to the middle of the span before they had time to react.

"I say!" Feobold's frantic warning reached Tym's ears even as a gobbling tried to bite one of them off. "Watch out! I'm not sure the bridge will take both of you. Even we gnomes cross it one by one. It's very old and a bit…"

With a splintering crash that sounded even above the roar of the torrent, the bridge collapsed.

"…fragile," concluded Feobold unhappily.

With a cry of despair, Tym fell into the raging blackness which drew him down, spinning him like a leaf. Ice-cold water gripped him and flooded his lungs. The river swept him away and darkness claimed him.

CHAPTER EIGHTEEN

How Tym and Colyn found themselves
All At Sea.

"**X**ut wiv the bad air, in wiv the good air: out wiv the
bad air, in wiv the good air…"

Tym awoke to find himself lying face down on pebbles.
He felt as if something had chewed him up and spat him out.
He coughed and spluttered feebly, and became aware that
there was a heavy weight on his back doing painful things to
his arms and shoulders.

"Out wiv the bad air, in wiv the good…"

"Get off!" Tym heaved his chest off the pebbles. Colyn,
who had been sitting on his back, fell back with a squawk.

"Well, there's gratitude for yer!" he complained, rubbing

the bits that Tym had deposited on the shingle. "I drag yer from a watery grave, an' what fanks do I get?"

Tym was coughing and sucking in great lungfuls of air. "What were you doing to me?" he demanded.

"Gettin' the water out of yer. Yer must've swallowed 'alf the river. I pumped out gallons an' gallons an' gallons…"

"It felt as if you were pulling my arms out of my sockets!"

"That's how yer do it," Colyn told him. "It's called Artificial Recreation."

Tym rather doubted this, but he was clearly still alive. He was still coughing up water and could feel plenty more sloshing around inside. "Where are we?" he asked.

"Well," said Colyn judiciously, "I'm not exackly sure, but the river carried us a long way, an' just down there it empties out into this lake that's so big you can't see across it. An' it's got waves an' big white birds that sound like cats, an' there's minnows in it that look like they could 'ave yer arm off, an' it's salty so I suppose – and, mind you, this is only a wild guess – I suppose it could be the sea."

Colyn had made a fire by rubbings bits of driftwood together at Whizzard speed. As the two of them sat beside it, trying to get dry, the little thief explained that the underground river had eventually emerged in a cave and then continued its flow above ground, becoming slower and wider as it did so. After a while, the water had started to taste of salt. Colyn had spotted Tym caught in a tangle of bushes and had managed to drag him to shore, where he had set about the task of resuscitating his companion.

"Aren't you supposed to do that mouth-to mouth these

days?" asked Tym, rubbing his aching arms.

Colyn gave him a wry look. "Yeah, well, no offence, but I thought I'd try the old way first."

"Well… thanks." Tym stood up and gazed over the biggest expanse of water he had ever seen. It had to be the sea. No lake could be this big. Even the birds that lived here were strange (Colyn was right, they did sound like cats): seagulls never flew as far inland as Dun Indewood. The sea itself was like a vast, restless animal, constantly hissing and crashing as its waves rolled up the shingle. Tym stared out over the shimmering waves. Light was spreading across the sky from the East, but dawn had not yet broken. The moon was rising over the sea. At least, *something* was rising over the sea.

"Colyn," called Tym, "we're a long way from home, aren't we?"

"I s'pose we must be," replied Colyn, getting up and coming to stand beside Tym.

"But even if we are a long way from home, do you think that the moon would be a different colour here?"

Colyn followed the direction of Tym's stare – and his jaw dropped. "It might change colour," he said slowly, 'but I reckon it would still be the same colour all the way across."

"Yes," said Tym, "that's what I thought. And I don't think the moon usually… billows like that."

The object of their speculation was round in shape. As it came closer, it took on the appearance of a football made by someone who was more used to making patchwork quilts – and it was big. Enormous, in fact. Its shape changed from moment to moment with a rippling movement. It seemed to have a network of ropes around it, like a spider's web, and dangling from them was something that looked like a basket.

Tym and Colyn had never seen a balloon; for that matter, they had never seen a ship. But they had seen the small boats that ferried people over the Trickle, and the shape that glided over the waves beneath the floating ball was clearly a much bigger version of those. It had three tall masts rather than the single, stumpy one usually found on boats that sailed the Trickle. Each mast was crossed with yards from which hung a great swell of sails, so that the ship looked as if it was being drawn along by its own captive cloud.

As they watched, the balloon was lowered on to the deck of the ship and its envelope collapsed. The sails suddenly lost their shape and flapped briefly before being gathered on to the yards by swarms of figures darting about in the rigging. With a rattle, something heavy on a chain dropped from the front end of the ship, which came to rest, riding easily on the waves. A few minutes later, boats were lowered. Oars flashing in the early light, their crews began to pull for the shore.

Tym licked lips that, in contrast to the rest of him, were suddenly dry. "We need a ship to cross the sea to the country of the Cumhera, so I suppose we should ask that one to take us."

Colyn said, "Yeah, we could. I daresay that black flag wiv the skull on it is just, like, an emblem…" The boats came nearer. "An' the fact that all the blokes on that boat 'ave got gold earrings an' teef missin' an' they're all waving nasty, sharp, curved swords an goin' 'Oo-arrr' a lot is just, you know, boyish high spirits. Probably very respectable folk when yer get to know 'em."

Tym shrugged unhappily. "Well, there's no point in being choosy. It might be ages before another ship comes." He waited with Colyn while the boats rode up on the shingle with a crunch. Their crews surrounded the boys, looking fierce and wary. Tym didn't like the look of the newcomers, but he tried to put them at ease with the seafaring talk he had learned from Captain Gorge. "Shiver the mainbrace and splice me barnacles, me hearties…" The ill-favoured crew looked at one another with puzzled expressions.

"What's he on about?"

"Danged if I know."

Tym tried again. "Ahoy, shipmates! Be you goin' a rovin' an' a wanderin' on the briny billows?"

The crew scratched their heads, dislodging an interesting collection of fleas and lice. "What'd he say?"

Tym gave an exasperated groan. "Look, we want to get to the other side of this sea. Can you take us?"

The pirates' expressions cleared. "Well, why didn't you say so?" demanded one who seemed to be in charge. He gave Tym and Colyn a friendly leer. "You'm welcome to join the crew of the good ship Oo-arrr."

Tym blinked. "The good ship *Oo-arrr*?"

"Aye. We call it that because it's the only word most of the crew can say."

"Oo-arrr!" agreed the ruffianly crew, leering horribly.

"I see," said Tym politely. "Will it be a long voyage?"

"No!" said the sailor with a wicked grin. He gave a nod

and two members of the crew who had crept round behind Tym and Colyn whalloped them expertly over the head with heavy, wooden belaying pins. "Just the rest of your lives," he added as the travellers slumped, unconscious, on to the shingle. The sailors cackled. "Not long at all."

A bucket of sea water in the face jerked Tym back into consciousness. He was becoming an expert at recovering from bangs on the head, Tym thought bitterly. It must be all the practice he was getting.

He lay on a heaving deck, feeling bruised and very sick. Clustered round him were a bunch of the ugliest-looking ruffians he had ever seen. Nearly every one had bits missing – an eye here, an ear there, an arm, a foot, a whole leg. They wore knotted handkerchiefs and tattered trousers with sashes, torn shirts or waistcoats. Some had bones stuck through their ears or noses, or plaited into their bedraggled hair or beards. They all smelt like polecats, and they were all armed to the teeth and leering horribly.

"You're pirates, ain't you?" Colyn, lying beside Tym, was struggling to sit up. He arranged an ingratiating smile on his face and held out his hand. "I'm a thief, meself. Pleased to meet yer."

Growling, one of the pirates raised a wicked looking curved sword. Colyn snatched his hand back hurriedly.

At that moment, a bellowed order rang across the deck.

"All hands make sail!" The pirates leapt for the rigging and swarmed up it. Those around Tym and Colyn signalled that they should do the same with savage cuffs and lashes from knotted ropes. Fleeing the stinging blows, Tym climbed up high above the deck and did his best to copy the other sailors who were loosening ties to allow the heavy sails to fall and catch the wind. Some distance below him, he saw Colyn doing the same.

After some minutes of agonising toil, the sails filled. The ship surged forward through the water. Tym looked down – and immediately wished he hadn't. The mast was swaying and the deck looked a very long way below. Tym gulped and clutched frantically at the ropes that lay along the top of the yard.

"Ouch!"

Tym turned his head – and stared. A small figure was gazing at him angrily. The creature was lashed to the yard with the rope that Tym had yanked on. It was about the size of a human child and its skin was blue. Its slim and graceful figure had a look of extreme lightness. Behind its back, two gauzy wings whirred rapidly, creating the draft which, Tym realised, was filling the sails.

"W-w-w-what are you?" Tym squeaked.

The small figure made a disgusted noise. "As if you didn't know, you clodhopping human." Its voice hissed like the sighing of wind through the treetops. "Isn't it enough that you enslave my brethren and I, and force us to power your gallumphing great galleon, without tugging on my bonds to torment me further?"

"I'm sorry," said Tym, "I didn't mean to hurt you. And I really don't know what you are. My friend and I were captured by the pirates on the shore over there." He pointed to the receding shoreline and nearly fell off the yard.

"Then you're a prisoner too?" The creature's eyes softened into an expression of weary unhappiness. "I am a sylph," it said sadly. It waved an arm to indicate the other yards, all of which, Tym now saw, were dotted with little bound figures, their wings whirring steadily. "Behold my unhappy brothers and sisters. We are spirits of the air. The pirates set snares for us and entrapped us. Now we are their slaves. We power their ship. We raise the balloon they use to spy for their victims."

Tym guessed that the strange creature was talking about the floating ball he and Colyn had seen. "Is that why they keep you tied up?" he asked. "So you won't fly away?"

The sylph nodded miserably. "Alas yes, even though there is no need. The pirates clip our wings; there is enough left for us to fan their sails, but not enough for us to fly away." The sylph stopped its wingbeats momentarily. Tym saw to his horror that the ends of its wings were torn and ragged. "Keeping us tied up is needless cruelty."

"They *are* cruel – cruel and wicked." Tym thought for a moment. "Look, my companion and I are prisoners, but we will help you, if we can – I promise."

At that moment, a thunder of drums echoed around the ship and shook the rigging. The pirates, suddenly panic-stricken, swarmed down to the deck, forcing Tym to accompany them so quickly it was a miracle he didn't fall.

Bumping and barging each other in their haste, the pirates formed rough lines from one side of the ship to the other, facing the raised deck to the rear. Wide-eyed with fear, they dragged Tym into line next to Colyn. Then there was silence, broken only by the creak of the rigging and an occasional whimper.

On the upper deck, one of the officers raised his voice. "Captain on deck! Make way for Queen Leysa!"

CHAPTER NINETEEN

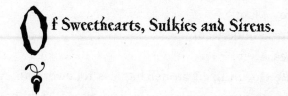

O f Sweethearts, Sulkies and Sirens.

A woman, well built and finely dressed in a red coat crossed with sword belts, strode on to the after-deck. Her face was scarred. She had a patch over one eye and a hook where her left hand should be.

"Captain Leysa?" Tym stared, thinking back to the evening in Luigi's restaurant that seemed so long ago. "That's never Captain Gorge's 'sweet little Leysa' is it?"

"Must be," hissed Colyn. "He always had lousy taste in women." Pirates on either side of Tym and Colyn cast furious glances at them and elbowed them in the ribs to be quiet.

Captain Leysa stepped up to the rail overlooking the lower

deck and swept the crew with an eye like a gimlet. The pirates quailed. "Now, my proud cut-throats!" The Pirate Queen spoke in a voice that growled and rasped like the sea on shingle. "My scourges of the seas, desperate devil-may-care buccaneers, pitiless scum of a thousand blood-soaked battles, tell me this: *have you brushed your teeth?*"

The pirates rolled their eyes and gibbered with terror. "Mum, yes, Mum!"

"And washed behind your ears?"

"Mum, yes, Mum!"

"Put on fresh underwear?"

"Mum, yes, Mum!"

The Pirate Queen fixed on her hapless followers an eye that flashed with unspeakable cruelty and hissed, "And have you all got clean handkerchiefs?"

Fumbling with ham-fisted ineptitude, the pirates reached into pockets and purses and pulled out snowy-white handkerchiefs which they waved frantically at their brutal commander.

The Pirate Queen stalked down each trembling line, inspecting handkerchiefs. Each pirate sagged with relief as his handkerchief passed muster. But suddenly, the Pirate Queen stopped dead in her tracks in front of one of her men. Tym craned his neck and saw that this pirate's hankie looked a good deal less clean than the others. She spiked the offending article on her hook and directed a look of utmost fury at its fainting owner.

"Slobbering Pete," she ground out, in a voice that could melt earwax, "what is this?"

"If you please, Mum." A friend of Slobbering Pete's, greatly daring, raised a quivering hand. "It's his slobberin', if you please. He can't help it. He mops up the slobber with his handkercher, please, Mum."

"That is no excuse!" The Pirate Queen's scorn caused tar to bubble out of the deck seams. "Thirty lashes of the cat!"

As Slobbering Pete was led away howling, Colyn caught the appalled look on Tym's face and whispered, "Don't worry, it's not a real cat. It's a whip called a cat-o'-nine-tails. I seen 'em in the torture chamber in the Castle, back in Dun Indewood."

A pirate scurried past them, carrying a bag that wriggled. A few moments later, from below decks, there came screams of agony, punctuated with furious meowing, yowling and spitting. "On the uvver 'and," said Colyn, turning a funny colour, "they do fings a bit different round 'ere."

The Pirate Queen had reached Tym and Colyn. She fixed on them a look of unbridled malevolence. "Where are your handkerchiefs?" she hissed.

"If you please, Ma'am…" Tym thought it best to be polite to this woman who clearly had en entire crew of merciless pirates in fear of their lives: "…we haven't got any."

"We're travellers," piped up Colyn. "From far away. Friends of Captain Gorge," he added with a wink at Tym. Colyn clearly thought that Gorge's name would have an effect on this dreadful woman. He was right – but not in a good way.

"*Captain Gorge?*" The Pirate Queen ground her teeth in fury. "Captain, indeed! That whey-faced poltroon! That scurvy swab who ran out on me – a poor, defenceless maid –

because he was too scared to face my father in a duel for my hand? May he rot in Davy Jones' locker while the fish nibble at his cowardly bones. So you're friends of his, are you?"

"Not exackly friends," Colyn backtracked quickly. "Mere acquaintances. Scarcely know 'im."

Captain Leysa grinned savagely. "Take them below! They can help our furry friends to heave on the sweeps!" Tym had no time to wonder what she meant. Rough hands grabbed him and they were hustled down into the bowels of the ship. One deck down... two... three. Tym and Colyn staggered into the gloom of the lowest deck of the vessel.

Here, just above the bilges, the air was rank and foetid. Rats could be heard, squeaking and scuttling about. As Tym's eyes adjusted to the gloom, he saw that there were rows of benches on either side of the ship. Each bench was occupied by two figures who sat slumped across long poles. Tym was manhandled down a raised platform between the benches and thrust on to one near the front of the ship. A pirate snapped manacles round his wrists and Tym was secured, unable to rise.

Tym peered into the gloom and saw that Colyn had been chained to a bench on the other side of the ship and a few rows down. He realised that there was another person sitting on the bench beside him. "What are we doing here?" he asked anxiously.

His companion turned great, sad, soulful eyes on Tym. "Don't ask," it said in a hopeless, bubbling voice that sounded like someone trying to speak while gargling with water. "Don't even think about it. It's too depressing."

Tym stared. The creature clearly wasn't human: its ears were small and set high on its head, its soup-plate eyes had long lashes and its flat nose, which overhung its mouth, had half a dozen or so bristly whiskers springing out on either side. Its body was covered with sleek, blue-grey fur and its fingers, resting on the pole in front of it, were webbed.

"You must have done something very bad," the creature said mournfully, "to be sent down here down here into the reeking dark to row with the sulkies."

"Row?" Tym suddenly realised that what he had thought was a pole was actually an oar. Tym turned to the creature beside him. "Are you a sulkie?"

"Well guessed," said the sulkie miserably. "Yes, we all are. Water sprites: seal-people. The pirates caught us in nets and carried us far from the cool, deep waters of our home. It's all just so unfair." It sobbed softly to itself. "We are a hardy folk and can row long after humans get tired. But eventually, in our sorrow, we pine and wither away to sea foam. That's something to look forward to, I suppose."

From all around them came a rattling of chains and a rumbling noise. "Open ports!" At the bellowed order, flaps in the side of the ship swung up and outwards. "Out sweeps!"

The sulkies stirred into life. They pushed their long oars out through the openings, and held them just above the waves. "Give way!"

As one, the sulkies dipped their oars into the water and heaved. Tym, matching his pace to that of his companion, pulled on his oar and saw Colyn doing the same. The sulkies worked their oars rhythmically, and began to sing to a steady, sad rhythm:

> "Deep and far, deep and far,
> Now lie our salt-sea caves.
> Our prison is a wooden shell
> That rides upon the waves.
> We heave the oars from dusk 'til dawn,
> From dawn 'til dusk again…
> Oh, weep for we poor sulkie folk
> Who live as slaves to men."

The sulkie turned to Tym. "Look on the bright side. If you die from exhaustion or some horrible disease, you won't be wrecked in a dreadful storm and your drowned corpse won't be torn to pieces on savage rocks, and what a mercy that will be." Then the morose creature burst into tears.

All the rest of that long and miserable day, Tym and Colyn rowed with the sulkies until their hands were blistered, their limbs ached and their backs felt as if they were broken in eight different places. With the combined power of the sylphs and the sulkies, the ship skimmed through the water at a furious rate.

When, at long last, the oars were shipped and the ports closed, Tym sank at once into an exhausted slumber. For the first time since he had left Dun Indewood, he found himself on the cold, desolate plain of the Dreamwalker's realm.

Zamarind was there. She gave a cry of relief on seeing him. "There you are! You haven't dreamt about me for ages! Where have you been?"

"*I'm sorry,*" said Tym glumly. "*I'm afraid I haven't had a lot of sleep lately, what with one thing and another.*"

"*Well, I have,*" said Zamarind tartly. Tym gave her a look of such misery that her face softened. "*I know you're trying to help,*" she said in a more friendly voice. "*The Dreamwalker has been letting me see what you've been getting up to. I'm afraid you've been having a rather rotten time.*"

"*That's one way of putting it…*"

"*Listen, I haven't got long. I expect they'll make you wake up to do some more rowing in a minute, and I've got a message for you. From the Dreamwalker. He said to tell you to remember the Sirens.*"

Tym frowned. "*Sirens?*"

"*You know, they're on the map.*"

"*I haven't got the map any more. I lost it when we fell into the land of the gnomes.*"

"*Oh, for pity's sake.*" Zamarind stamped her foot impatiently. "*Just tell the pirates that there's treasure on the island five leagues to the North-east.*"

She began to fade. Tym cried, "*Wait!*"

But a pirate boot in the ribs jerked him awake and his dream vanished. He looked up into a face that, even by pirate standards, was exceptionally ugly.

"Cap'n wants to see you," growled the hideous rogue, unshackling him. Tym stumbled along the gangway to join Colyn who had also been freed.

"They're probably going to hang you," called Tym's rowing companion. "Still, it's better than being eaten by sharks. Count your blessings."

Moments later, Tym and Colyn were shoved into the captain's cabin, much in the way that a zookeeper might push a haunch of meat into the cage of a starving tiger.

"Well, me buckoes." Captain Leysa was smoking a cigar the size of a cucumber. Tym's eyes streamed in its smoke. "Let's see if a spell on the sweeps has loosened your tongues. Suppose you tell me what you're doing on my ship."

Tym had been thinking furiously on the way to the cabin. "We came to seek the treasure of the Cumhera," he said boldly. At his side, Colyn gave an involuntary twitch at this barefaced lie; but, being an accomplished liar himself, said nothing. He had no idea what Tym had in mind, but he was ready to back him up.

The Pirate Queen gave a bark of laughter. "Then you're mad! Many have tried and failed! Their bones litter the desert where the beast roams."

Tym gave her a calculating look. "Many men would risk all, for such treasure."

Captain Gorge's 'sweet little Leysa' spat with such power and accuracy that she knocked the ship's clock off the cabin wall. "Men! Weak, pitiful creatures! All they ever do is boast and belch and leave the seat up on the privy! Where would this crew be without Cap'n Leysa to see that they clip their toenails regular and change their socks once a month, eh? And you speak of treasure! Hah!"

Leysa leapt to her feet, pulling at a silver chain around her well-muscled neck. A silver key dangled at the end of it. She strode across the cabin and unlocked a stout wooden door. Colyn's eyes bulged at the display of gold and jewels that lay inside the Pirate Queen's strongroom. His mouth watered. "What think you of that?" demanded Leysa harshly. "The plunder of a thousand battles, two thousand wrecks. Is that not a treasure indeed?"

Tym sniffed. "Very nice. But compared to the Cumhera's treasure, this is a trifle."

The Pirate Queen looked daggers at him. "You're an insolent fool. Guard!" She threw open the cabin door. The guard tumbled into the room. He had been listening at the door, as Tym had hoped he would. It made his next task easier. Tym barely listened as Captain Lesya ordered the pirate to return the prisoners to the lower deck. He was too busy planning the next part of his scheme.

As soon as the captain's door had shut, Tym said to Colyn, "She never asked us how we planned to take the Cumhera's treasure. Shame. Now, she'll never know."

The guard guffawed, but there was a greedy glint in his eye. "Had a plan, did you, matey? What would that be then?"

Tym sighed. "Oh, just to use the Helmet of Invisibility. But that doesn't matter now."

The pirate looked around cautiously and asked, in an offhand sort of way, "What Helmet of Invisibility be this, shipmate?"

"The one that… no," said Tym, "I can tell you're not really interested."

In a flash, the pirate's sea-knife was at Tym's throat. "Come on, matey," growled the pirate. "Tell old Throatslitter Ted."

"Well – all right," said Tym with every appearance of

reluctance. "It's on the Island of the Sirens."

Throatslitter Ted cleared his throat nervously. "The Island of the Sirens? Cap'n do say that place be too dangerous to go near."

"Well, she would, wouldn't she?" said Tym offhandedly. "What would happen if one of her men – you, for instance – got hold of the Helmet of Invisibility? How long would Leysa be captain for then, I wonder?"

Ted's eyes glinted, but he said, "That's mutinous talk, that is!"

"Have it your own way. You'd better just take us back to our oars then."

"As a matter of interest – 'ow far be this island, matey?"

"Five leagues to the North-east," said Tym promptly. Colyn boggled.

Ted's eyes darted about uncertainly. "I daresn't go against Cap'n…"

"Of course not. You like having to brush your teeth and wash behind your ears, do you?"

Throatslitter Ted growled deep in his throat. "And how would a man find this helmet, supposin' he was lookin' for it?"

"He wouldn't," said Tym sharply. "We'd have to show him where it is. If someone had a mind to go and find the helmet, he might forget to lock our manacles. Then when he reached the island, he'd only have to come below and fetch us, and we could lead him straight to the helmet." He gave Ted a knowing wink.

"That's enough chat!" Throatslitter Ted pushed Colyn and

Tym down the companionway and thrust them roughly into their seats in the bowels of the ship. But he didn't lock their manacles and he gave Tym a quick, confidential wink when he left. Colyn cast a look back at Tym, but they were too far apart to talk without the risk of being heard, so he said nothing.

Some time later, Tym felt the ship slowly begin to turn. At a whispered order, the oar ports were opened, slowly and quietly. A pirate crept along the gangway, hissing that the oars were to be deployed but that the rowers were not to make a sound. Tym guessed that the pirates had fallen in with his plan and were being very careful that Captain Leysa didn't find out.

It must have been well after midnight when Tym heard a panic-stricken cry from above. He threw off his shackles and turned to the sulkie beside him. "Keep rowing," he hissed and shifted to Whizzard speed.

Colyn leapt up. The Whizzard and his companion pounded along the gangway between the suddenly still ranks of rowers, up on to the moonlit deck. They tumbled into one of the ship's boats and slowed to normal speed...

Ahead lay an island, from which a flashing blue light bathed the ship in bursts of unearthly brilliance. An eerie wail rose and fell, howling mournfully on the wind. "*OOOOeeeeOOOOeeeeOOOOeeee…*" All around, pirates moaned in terror.

"They'm comin' for us!"

"They know we'm in here!"

"They'll never take us alive!"

Colyn stared at the fear-crazed pirates. "Wot's up wiv them?"

Tym thought hard. "I suppose they're scared of the Sirens because they know they've done wrong."

Colyn considered. "I ain't scared of them."

"Maybe you're too young. Anyway, you never think you *have* done wrong!"

Colyn grinned. "True!"

Captain Leysa burst on deck with curlers in her hair and a buckler strapped over her nightdress. "What in thunder is going on, you swabs?" She saw the blue light and gave a gasp of horror. "Fools! Didn't I tell you? 'Tis the black madness that falls on any man who goes too near the Sirens!"

But the crew were too crazed with fear to listen. Howling with terror, they turned the ship, desperate to flee from the eerie lights and blood-curdling wails. Leysa was knocked to the deck as her men stampeded over her in their panic. The ship curved away from the island – and towards the dreadful reefs that lurked nearby. At full speed, with a crash like the end of the world, the pirate ship flung itself on to the razor sharp rocks and began to sink.

CHAPTER TWENTY

How the Ship Went Down and the
Balloon Went Up.

Tym and Colyn shot to Whizzard speed. Breaking waves
hovered over the doomed vessel. Pirates, caught in mid-
stagger (and mid-scream) achieved impossible angles of lean.

"Where's the guard?" Tym scanned the faces on the
quarter-deck, looking for the repulsive features of Throatslitter
Ted. "There he is!" Ted was falling backwards through a
broken section of rail. Tym slithered down towards him and
snatched the keys from the pirate's belt. He half turned –
hesitated – then reached out and pulled the pirate back from
the brink, wrapping the man's arms round an undamaged
section of rail. As an afterthought, he snatched the pirate's

dagger from his belt and slid it down inside his own boot. Then he climbed back up the sloping deck to meet Colyn.

"I'm going to release the sulkies," he said. "You climb up the rigging and untie the sylphs."

Colyn was flushed with excitement but the look he gave Tym was apprehensive. "Yeah. Then what?"

"Then we'll escape in one of the ship's boats."

"Aye aye, Cap'n." Giving Tym an uneasy echo of his normal, cheeky grin, Colyn scrambled up the rigging. Tym spun round and went below.

At Whizzard speed, the noise of the storm was a dull roar, featureless but still deafening. The splinter of smashing timbers sounded like thunderclaps. Tym pushed his way past the unresisting bodies of terrified pirates, all climbing, falling, swarming over each other in their desperation.

Tym reached the lower deck and gave a gasp of horror. A wall of water was breaking through the shattered sides of the ship. Even at Whizzard speed the great mass was heaving forward inch by inch. The great wooden hull was splintering under the pressure. It was a race against time.

Tym set to work releasing the sulkies from their manacles. It was an agonisingly slow process. He had no way of knowing which key would release which lock. He fumbled desperately at the keyholes. Sometimes he was lucky and found the right key straightaway but more often than not, he was forced to try every key in every set.

As Tym raced from lock to lock, the sea inched into the ship through great gashes in the rapidly disintegrating hull. The water level rose slowly but inexorably. It had reached above the heads of the rowers nearest the stern before he'd finished. Tym was forced to dive again and again into the freezing water. At last, with lungs bursting, he released the last of the seal-people. He swam to the wooden stairs, held on to the rail and slowed to normal speed.

The sea gushed in, covering the sulkies and buffeting Tym about. One of the sulkies (he thought it was his rowing companion) swam to Tym's side with easy strokes. "I suppose we have you to thank for freeing us from our chains." Tym could only nod. The sulkie gave him a whiskery kiss on both cheeks. "My people are in your debt."

"Will they all be all right?" Tym managed to gasp. "Some of them were under water for a long time."

"My people breathe more easily below the water than above it."

Tym hadn't thought of that! "Then I needn't have released you after all," he blurted. He stared round at the sulkies who were tearing at the broken timbers of the hull, clearing passages to the open sea.

The sulkie shook its head like a wet dog. "If you had not, we should have remained shackled to this ship. We should have starved to death, or been eaten by sharks. Of course, we're a long way from home and what with giant seasnakes and killer whales and octopuses, I don't suppose we'll ever get back there. Hardly worth your while to rescue us really. Nevertheless, we shall not forget."

Tym almost laughed.

"Now, save yourselves. Of course, you'll probably die of

thirst on some barren island or get eaten by cannibals in a day or two. Still, that's life. Farewell." The sulkie dived beneath the rising waters.

Dripping and staggering as the stricken vessel lurched, Tym climbed up through the ship. He was just about to set foot on the final staircase to the open air, when a strong arm grasped him round the neck. He felt the sting of a wickedly sharp hook-point beneath his ear.

"Wretched meddler!" growled the voice of Captain Leysa. "I'll warrant this is all your doing. I shall slit your weasand!"

At last, thought Tym, I'm going to find out where my weasand is. Pity Colyn'll miss it. He closed his eyes.

There was a thud. The arm around his neck went limp. And there was Colyn, peering down the hatchway. He was still holding the wooden keg he had brought down with all his strength on the Pirate Queen's head. "I untied all the sylphs," he said, grinning at Tym's astonished face. "Shall we go now?"

Tym lunged for the stairway – and a hand grasped his foot. He kicked out and hauled himself upwards. Just in time. With an inhuman scream of rage, Leysa erupted from the hatch like an avenging fury. Strapped around her were bags – canvas holdalls, leather scrips and purses, saddlebags: all were bulging and some were half open, showing the glint of gold and the sparkle of precious stones inside.

Tym and Colyn stood rooted to the spot. Leysa's eyes were wide with madness, her wickedly sharp hook sliced through the air as she sought to rip the Whizzard and his companion apart. Captain Leysa lunged forward – and was flung aside by the mainmast which, snapped in two at last by the buffeting of the waves, fell across the deck, sweeping the Pirate Queen into the raging sea.

Tym ran to the rail and peered down. Leysa was struggling to stay afloat, but the treasure was pulling her under. "Leysa!" Tym's cry almost tore his throat. "Leysa! You'll drown! Let the bags go!"

The woman stared up at him, eyes blazing with insane pride. "Give up my treasure? Never! Nev..." But at that moment, the waves closed over her head for the last time.

"'Ere."

At the sound of Colyn's voice, Tym tore his eyes away from the spot where Leysa had disappeared. "Yes?"

"You know them ships' boats we was goin' to escape in?"

"Yes?"

"Would those be the same boats that are rowin' away the other side of those rocks?"

"*What?*" Colyn was right. Tym peered through the blinding spray at the escaping crew and felt a numbing sense of failure.

A sylph fluttered to his side. "You are troubled. What is the matter?"

"The matter? Hah!" Tym clenched his fists. "I'm sorry. All the boats have gone. I've doomed us all."

"Not yet," hissed the sylph. "There is still a way. Come."

Using its ragged wings to balance on the crazily tilting deck, the slender creature led the way to the quarter-deck where a group of its fellows were unpacking the observation balloon.

"But you can't fly," protested Tym, "and we can't swim. How can any of us get away?"

"There is more than one way to fly."

Several sylphs crawled under the edge of the balloon. Tym could see them burrowing beneath the particoloured envelope like small boys under a blanket. Suddenly, the material of the balloon began to bulge – and gradually grew higher and rounder as they watched.

The sylph by their side chuckled with a voice like the wind blowing through reeds. "Sylphs have their wings, but they also have their breath. Their breath is lighter than the wind. They are filling the balloon." More sylphs joined in and the balloon inflated rapidly, rising as it did so. The ship lurched and settled further on the rocks. Tym looked down at the dark, foaming water. It would be touch and go.

The balloon left the deck. Tym and Colyn dived headfirst into the basket. The final sylphs swarmed up the lines that fastened the basket to the balloon, and up into the envelope by the great vent above the basket. Tym looked up and saw tens of sylphs, hanging from a network of lines inside the balloon, blowing for all they were worth. The basket left the deck just as the ship, with a last groan of rending timbers, began to slip beneath the waves.

"The ropes!" cried the sylph who had joined them in the basket. "Cut the ropes!" Tym understood. The sinking vessel was dragging the balloon down into the angry sea. With a burst of Whizzard speed, Tym pulled the pirate's dagger from his boot and hacked at the guyropes. One by one they parted. As Tym returned to normal speed, the balloon lifted clear. As the bowsprit of the pirate ship sank beneath the waves, its balloon, captive no longer, rose proudly over the turbulent sea to be bathed in the first rays of the rising sun.

The balloon flew on in the crisp morning air. They had risen above the level of the clouds, which now lay below them, white and fat, like lazy sheep in a meadow. Below the clouds lay the rippling waters of the sea. There was no land in sight.

As Tym began to feel safer, he had fallen into a deep sleep. Now he lay curled up against the wickerwork of the basket, snoring gently.

Tym's dreaming self stood on the desolate plain. Zamarind was facing him. Tym was shocked to see her dream-figure looking thin and frail, almost transparent, as if a breath of wind would blow her away.

She said, "*I don't think I will be alive much longer.*"

"*I know.*" Tym's voice was despondent. "*I'm going as fast as I can. I think we must be nearly at the Cumhera's country.*"

"*Please be quick.*" There was a catch in Zamarind's voice. "*I get very frightened, just lying in bed. Grandfather spends a lot of time with me, and Nursie, and Humfrey and the Runemaster come by sometimes and stand around shaking their heads, but all the doctors and the other wizards never come at all now. I think they've given up on me.*"

"*I haven't!*" said Tym, more boldly than he felt.

Zamarind gave him a watery smile, but Tym could see she had little faith in him. Well, why should she? he asked himself bitterly.

Then, suddenly, the Dreamwalker was with them, outlined against the black sky. The great creature turned its star-filled eyes on Tym. "*You have done well,*" it said in a softer voice than Tym had heard it use before.

Tym shook his head. "*I should have been concentrating on getting to the Cumhera as soon as possible. Instead, I wasted time helping the Gnome Prince, and the sylphs, and the sulkies…*"

"*Think you so?*" The Dreamwalker gave Tym a searching look. "*Count no time wasted that you have spent in the service of fellow creatures. And who knows? Your new friends may yet have a part to play, before the end…*"

"There! There!" A sylph's cry roused Tym from his dream. The air-creature was standing on the rim of the basket, one hand on the rigging, the other pointing into the distance. Its wings were fluttering with excitement.

Tym scrambled up. Below, the blue of the sea was changing to pale brown as their flight took them across the coast and over the land. Then he peered in the direction of the sylph's pointing finger. At first, he saw nothing; then he spotted a plume of flame on the horizon. Tym shrugged. "A fire. So what?"

"No ordinary fire!" The sylph danced about on the rim of the basket as Colyn struggled, bleary-eyed, to his feet. "The fires of the Cumhera! Our way home!"

Tym stared. "The Cumhera?" He shuddered. It looked as if their quest was nearing its end. He wasn't at all sure he felt ready.

"Yes." The sylph's voice became more serious. "Four great flames burn around the treasure of the Cumhera, and warm air rises. Even with our clipped wings, we can ride the air currents to the upper reaches of the sky. Above the flames, we can fly again, until our wings have healed and grown stronger, and the freedom of the air is ours once more."

"Then you have found what you seek," said Tym. "And so have we. We came here to find the Cumhera."

The flames grew brighter as the balloon travelled towards them over the barren land of the Cumhera. Tym and Colyn watched with increasing apprehension as the flames became four vast columns, stabbing high into the air.

The sylph pointed. "There is the Cumhera's lair." Its wings trembled in anticipation. "We must prepare to leave the balloon as we approach the flames. We dare not overshoot them, for if we go too far, we will be unable to fly in the cooler air and easy prey for the Cumhera itself. And once we leave the balloon, it will fall to the ground like a stone."

Tym gritted his teeth. "Very well," he said. "Let us down as gently as you can." The balloon began a curved descent towards the desert sands. As the fiery columns loomed, Tym and Colyn braced themselves.

The sylph reached out its hand. "Let me have your knife," it pleaded. Tym drew the dagger and passed it to the creature.

Tym turned to Colyn. "We'd better get ready to jump," he said tightly. Colyn looked terrified. The sylph bowed to Tym. Then it hurried up the ropes and into the balloon. Tym watched it climbing through the ranks of its fellows into the top of the envelope.

After that, there was no time for thought. The balloon was still travelling towards the flames at a steady pace. At the last moment, the sylphs inside the balloon made an extra effort, so that the balloon levelled out not far above the ground. Tym took a deep breath – and jumped.

He fell on to sand that wasn't nearly as soft as it looked. When he'd stopped rolling, Tym lay winded and gasping for breath. He was just congratulating himself that he seemed to have escaped serious hurt when Colyn landed on top of him.

Tym pushed Colyn away and stared groggily upwards. Free of their weight, the balloon had risen quickly and now a vast rent appeared in the upper part. Through this, the sylphs streamed out with joyous cries. Then the balloon crashed to the ground and began to disintegrate as the desert wind dragged it across the sand.

Tym and Colyn sat stunned, getting their breath back and rubbing their bruises. Over their heads, the sylphs rose above the fire columns, their mutilated wings catching the updraft as they returned to the air that was their element and their home. They flew up and up, spiralling high above, blue sparks among the red, until they finally disappeared from sight.

CHAPTER TWENTY-ONE

How Colyn caused a Flaming Row and how the Scales were Turned.

Tym and Colyn staggered to their feet and looked around. From four holes in the ground flared the four great pillars of flame, shooting ceaselessly into the air and roaring like caged beasts. To one side of them was the huge statue of a strange and outlandish creature. Its goat's body, wrapped about by its scaly serpent's tail, lay with its legs curled beneath it, while its lion's head reared up proudly, staring out across the desert.

It also looked out over something else. Between the four columns of flame, stacked in a regular mound, stood a greater collection of treasure than either Tym or Colyn had ever dreamed possible. Gold glinted in the firelight: gold coins, gold ornaments, candlesticks, crowns. Glinting among the gold were precious stones: glowing green emeralds, deep red rubies, cold sapphires and amethysts, the sparkling white of great diamonds.

Colyn roamed around the pile, marvelling at the wealth displayed. "Don't touch anything," Tym warned.

Colyn gave him a hurt look. "Wot d'you take me for?"

"A thief," Tym said evenly. "You told me so yourself."

"That's right, give a dog a bad name." Colyn folded his arms and sulked.

Tym sighed and turned away from the statue, scanning the desert. "Well, we've found the treasure. Now all we have to do is wait for the Cumhera to turn up."

"*If* it does." Colyn's voice was scornful. "I daresay that's just a load of old wives' tales. People see the fires from way off, an' the statcher, an' they fink there's a real beast called the Cumhera wot breathes fire. I bet there's no such fing."

"Do you really think so?" said a voice in his ear.

Tym spun round. Colyn, on the opposite side of the treasure, stood as unmoving as any person caught out of time by Whizzard speed. After a long pause, he said. "Tym…"

Goggling as if his eyes would pop and hardly daring to breathe, Tym squeaked, "Yes?"

"This isn't a statcher behind me, is it? It's the Cumhera."

"That's right," said Tym carefully.

Colyn's voice rose several octaves and cracked. "Why didn't anyone ever tell us how *big* it was?"

The Cumhera rose gracefully on its slender legs. Colyn backed carefully away. The creature stepped daintily forward on its goat's hooves and its serpent tail swished. In a voice as flat and dry as the desert itself, it spoke: "What make you in my domain, humans?"

Tym felt as if his legs were suddenly made of Luigi's spaghetti, but his voice hardly shook as he replied, "We came to ask you for a boon."

"I think not." The Cumhera's tail twitched angrily. "I think you came to steal my treasure."

"You're wrong," called Tym boldly. "We do not desire your treasure. We are not thieves!"

"Is that so?" The gigantic creature bent its head and fixed Colyn with an implacable gaze. "What have you hidden in your tunic?"

Shamefaced, Colyn reached inside his jerkin – and pulled out a diamond as big as a pigeon's egg. He shot Tym an apologetic glance. "Sorry. Couldn't resist it."

Tym stared at him with a look of horrified betrayal. The Cumhera crouched like a cat about to spring, and spoke again. "You were unwise to come here. All those who attempt to steal from my treasure must face me in a fair fight – to the death!"

The creature took a deep breath. A split second before it shot out a jet of fire to incinerate him where he stood, Tym went to Whizzard speed.

"Right," said Colyn, "you grab the scale an' then—" He broke off. The Cumhera was moving!

It blasted its jet of fire at Tym, who rolled aside at the last moment and felt it singe the soles of his feet. "Look out!" he yelled. "It can move at Whizzard speed, too."

Colyn gulped. "Well, the Runemaster said it was fast."

Tym dodged another jet of fire. "What do we do now?"

"I reckon this is time fer the old pincer movement." Colyn skipped out of the way as the Cumhera directed its fiery breath at him. The beast lunged back towards Tym. "You attract its attention, I'll get the scale."

Tym dived, rolled and came up running as the sand of the desert fused into glass behind him. "I've got a better idea. *You* attract its attention and I'll get the scale!"

"Just go for the scale if you get the chance!"

Tym and Colyn found themselves on opposite sides of the Cumhera – which was the best place for them to be; the Cumhera was trying to watch and attack both of them at once, and the time it took to swing its great head and body between them gave them time to dodge. When it attacked Tym, its tail was exposed to Colyn, and vice versa. But the wretched beast was very quick and its fiery breath was lethal.

An idea came to Tym. As the Cumhera was turning back towards Colyn, he yelled, "Hey, snake-tail! What are you getting so excited about? I bet you stole this treasure yourself anyway."

With a hiss of fury, the Cumhera swung back to face him. "You lie!" it roared.

"What? You mined the gold? You dug out the gems? *Puh*lease!" Out of the corner of his eye, Tym saw that Colyn was sneaking up on the creature. A few more seconds! "Tell the truth! The treasure was never yours in the first place, was it? *NOW, COLYN!*"

Tym dived aside as the Cumhera shot a jet of flame towards him. The creature turned its head just as Colyn reached out to snatch a scale. With a contemptuous flick of its tail, the Cumhera caught the young thief and sent him flying through the air to land with a thump on the hard sand some distance away, winded and outmanoeuvred.

Tym racked his brains. This wasn't working. The creature was not only fast, it was clever too. It turned towards Colyn – in desperation, Tym ran to the treasure hoard and stood before it.

"Hey! Smokey!" Tym grabbed a crown from the hoard and put it on his head, tilted to at insolent angle. "I'm stealing your treasure! So flame me!" The giant guardian of the treasure regarded him balefully. "You can't do it, can you? You'll melt all these precious things."

"Perhaps not," said the Cumhera. It drew back its lips, revealing an impressive display of dentistry. "But I have teeth as well as fire."

It lunged at Tym, who dropped the crown and ran for his life. But a diamond, accurately thrown, hit the creature in the eye. It reared up, waving its hooves in front of its face. Colyn gave a cackle of laughter.

Tym smiled to himself. His ruse had given his companion time to recover, but the Cumhera wouldn't fall for the same trick twice. There had to be a way to outwit it – there had to be…

And then the answer came to him. A pincer movement,

yes, but not only in space. A pincer movement in *speed*. The Cumhera had weapons at both ends. It could beat off attacks from two directions at once... but not from two speeds at once. Not if it meant what it had said about a fair fight.

Tym thought fast. There was no way of communicating his plan to Colyn; he would just have to hope that the thief would be quick enough on the uptake to get the idea. It was a gamble, but it should get them what they'd come for – if Tym was right.

If he was wrong, he'd be a small cloud of greasy smoke in about three seconds.

Crossing his fingers, Tym willed himself out of Whizzard speed. Slow... slower... slowest...

The Cumhera and Colyn disappeared. Now he had slowed to normal speed he could no longer see them. Tym kept his fingers crossed and waited. Would the Cumhera keep its word? He would know soon enough – or he would never know anything, ever again.

Seconds later, the Cumhera reappeared. "What are you doing, human?" it asked in its expressionless voice. "Did you think thus to escape me?"

"No," said Tym, almost with regret. "I had to trust that you were a creature of honour: that when I slowed to my normal speed, you would not flame me where I stood, for you promised me a fair fight. And so you, too, slowed to normal speed..."

The Cumhera gave a great cry and reared up, flailing at the air with its hooves.

"...but my companion didn't," grinned Tym.

The Cumhera stood before him, its great eyes still angry –
but now, it seemed to Tym, sad as well. It gave a single sigh.
Then it slowly toppled over, landing with a mighty thud that
shook the earth and sent the sand shooting up in clouds.
Tym stared at it in astonishment and horror.

Then Colyn appeared, waving an iridescent scale
triumphantly. "I got it, Tym! I saw what you was at, an' I
sneaked in an'…" Colyn stopped and followed Tym's
horrified gaze. "Lumme! What's up with it?"

Tym shook his head. "I don't know." Cautiously, he
approached the fallen creature. The great eyes swivelled to
follow him, but the Cumhera did not move.

"The treasure is yours, human. Much good may it do
you." The creature's voice was as expressionless as ever, but
faint now. Speaking seemed to pain it. "By taking my scale
you have given me my death wound."

Colyn stared at the scale on his hand. "Go on! I only took
a little one!"

"I don't want the treasure," blurted Tym. "I needed the
scale, but I never meant to harm you!"

"What is this – remorse from a thief?"

"I'm not a thief. At least, I never meant to be one. I need
your scale to save someone's life. I didn't take it for myself."

"Does that make it right?"

"I don't want you to die!" cried Tym. "What can I do?"

The Cumhera's voice was barely audible. "There is only
one way you can restore me to life. Burn my scale. Sacrifice it
to the fire by which I have my being. Only then can I rise
again." The Cumhera's great eyes filmed over. The pillars of

fire around its treasure began to falter, burning lower and lower...

Tym turned away. For several minutes he said nothing. Then he reached out his hand. "Give me the scale."

"You're off your nut!" Colyn was horrified. "You're free pearls short of a necklace! Wot are you finkin' of? You're never finkin' of burnin' the scale? Look at what we went through to get it! What about the Lady Zamarind, eh?"

Tym turned to him a face that was streaked with tears. "I can't help that. This isn't right. *'Be true to your true self.'* I know what I have to do. It doesn't matter that it's not what I want."

"What? You're gonna save the Cumhera? Bring it back to life? What for? So it can try to kill us again?"

"We came to its country," said Tym. "We tried to steal its treasure."

"Pull the other one." Colyn waved his arms about in agitation. "How did it get that treasure, eh? You said it yourself! Did it make it, or buy it? No – it nicked it, from all over the Forest – an' how many people did it kill to get it? Anyfink we done to it, it's done worse!"

Tym shook his head angrily. "We don't know that. Anyway, it doesn't matter. However it came by its hoard, I have to put right the damage that I have done. Whatever the Cumhera may or may not have done to gather its treasure, its death is on my head."

"Fine!" Colyn stamped his feet in a passion. "Wonderful! Perfect! We travel a thousand miles to get a scale of the Cumhera, an' now we've got it you're goin' to burn it. Good idea! Go ahead!"

Tym approached the nearest dying column of flame, now little more than his own height. "Sorry, Zamarind," he whispered. He held the scale for a moment – then cast it into the fire where it flashed into nothingness.

And the pillars of fire leapt up again, higher than before. Their golden glow bathed the surrounding desert. Motes of light, which might have been sparks, flowed from the flames and surrounded the still form of the Cumhera, bathing its coat in lines of fire. The creature's ribcage stirred, the lids flickered and its eyes glinted. Then the Cumhera blinked, rolled slowly over, and sat up.

"It was shamming," growled Colyn. "I told you. Fancy falling for that one. The oldest trick in the book."

The Cumhera regarded Tym steadily.

"So what do we do now? Wait for it to attack us again? Then what'll the plan be, great master?" Colyn was watching the gigantic beast with an expression in which wariness and fury were curiously mingled. He was also ready to bolt.

But when the Cumhera finally spoke, its voice was mild. "You restored me to life."

Without triumph, without regret, Tym said, "Yes."

"But why, if you had need of my scale?"

The emptiness of Tym's voice matched the Cumhera's. "I sought your scale to undo a wrong, but in taking it I found I'd done a greater wrong. I did the first wrong by accident: the second was by design. One wrong can't make another right. I've failed in my quest, because I can't succeed in it without doing a worse evil than I did at its start. Kill me, if that is your wish."

The Cumhera drew back its lion's lips, and bared its terrible lion's teeth... and, twisting its long neck, reached back over its body. With great care, it closed its teeth over a single scale of its tail, which it plucked out and dropped on to the sand at Tym's feet.

Tym stared at it, stunned. "But you'll die!" he whispered.

The Cumhera shook its huge head. "No. A theft is one thing. A gift, deserved and freely given, is a different matter entirely. A theft will kill me: a gift only makes me stronger." Tym saw that the wound left from the missing scale had already healed and a new scale grown to replace it.

Colyn gave a shout of joy and slapped Tym on the back with a force that made him stagger (keeping one eye watchfully on the Cumhera as he did so).

Tym was speechless. The words "Thank you" seemed feeble and inadequate, but he said them anyway and the Cumhera nodded regally. Then it stalked to the far side of the treasure and resumed the position it had been in when Tym and Colyn had found it, gazing out across the desert as if nothing had ever happened.

Tym gave Colyn an appraising look. "We'd better make a start. We have a long way to go – and I'll feel a lot better when we put some distance between your itchy fingers and the temptation of that hoard!" Fast... faster... fastest...

It was evening as the Whizzard and his companion reached the seashore. Tym felt almost carefree for the first time in many days. The run had eased his mind and the quest was accomplished after all. All they had to do was get the Cumhera's scale back to Zamarind and...

Tym felt himself slowing. He willed himself to go faster... and continued to lose speed. Ahead of him, Colyn looked back. "Come on, slowcoach! What's keepin' you?" Tym saw his expression change as he, too, began to slow down. "Hey! What's goin' on?"

Tym ground to a halt. He threw himself face down on to the desert sand, gave way to despair. "The potion!" he cried. "Our Whizzard potion! It's worn off!"

Colyn's eyes opened wide in horror. "But that means... we'll never get the Cumhera's scale back to Dun Indewood in time to save the Lady Zamarind."

Tym nodded. "We have the scale, but we've still lost." His voice was dull and lifeless. "We've failed after all."

Chapter Twenty-Two

H ow Herbit Helped Himself and Tym
Dreamed Up a Solution.

T hey sat on the seashore, hunched up, staring as if wishes
could bridge the hundreds of weary miles to Dun Indewood.
Colyn moodily flicked small pebbles into the waves. There
seemed nothing else to do. At least it was cooler here, and
there was a little fresh water – just a bitter trickle oozing out
of the rocks near the sea's edge, but enough to wet their
parched throats after the final hot trudge across the desert.

The sea was bright blue, placid and empty of ships.
Occasionally, a lizard or beetle would scramble across the
burning sand. Apart from these, the two boys might have
been the only things left alive in the world.

As the last rays of the sun disappeared, Colyn shivered and said, "Well? Wot are we goin' to do now?"

"I don't know about you," said Tym, "but I'm going to go to sleep."

Colyn gave him a disgusted look. "Oh, very helpful! How can you sleep at a time like this?"

"Because it's our only chance." Tym lay on his back and tried to relax. "There's only one person who can help us now. I'm going to meet him."

Tym closed his eyes. Colyn shook his head. "Mad as a mashed potato," he muttered under his breath. "It's all that sun. Boiled 'is brains." He threw another pebble.

"Colyn?"

"Yeah?"

"Stop throwing pebbles."

"Well, pardon me!" Colyn stomped off and sat further down the beach, sulking. The last of the light faded from the sky. Small waves broke on the sand with a soft hiss. Tym let the sound lull him to sleep.

Slowly, the faint figure of the Dreamwalker materialised before Tym. It was kneeling, its hands cupped on the ground in front of it.

"*Dreamwalker!*" cried Tym, "*I need your help!*" Then a feeling of dread washed over him. "*Where is Zamarind?*"

The Dreamwalker gazed at him. The stars of its eyes seemed to be burning less brightly than before, as though sorrow had dimmed them. The Dreamwalker whispered, "*We are losing her…*"

The great figure opened its cupped hands, revealing

Zamarind sitting on the cold floor of the desert. Her eyes were wide and frightened. Tym cried her name and stepped forward, but she gave no sign of having seen or heard him. She opened her mouth to speak and the sound that emerged was like the crying of a night-bird, with no words at all.

"*She has lost her way even in my world,*" said the Dreamwalker sadly. "*Soon she will fade altogether, unless you return and restore her.*"

"*I can't!*" Tym was almost weeping with misery and frustration. "*I've lost my Whizzard speed. The potion's worn off. I'm stuck on the wrong side of the sea. What can I do? Unless you can help me, I have no hope at all!*"

"*I, help you?*" The Dreamwalker nodded slowly. "*Perhaps I can.*"

It began to sing – the sort of soft, formless humming that mothers sing to lull their infants to sleep. After a while, a figure began to materialise.

It had the semi-transparent form of all who visited the Dreamwalker's plain, but Tym recognised it. "*Feobold!*" he called.

The Gnome Prince, who had been staring around dumbfounded, looked up sharply. His face split into a smile of recognition. "*My friend! Well met! But what is this place?*" He looked up at the great figure of the Dreamwalker with awe and some apprehension.

The Dreamwalker continued to hum and a second figure appeared – a sylph, who seemed, by its delighted greeting, to be the creature that had guided them to the balloon. Tym was pleased to see that its wings already looked less ragged and torn. It hovered above Feobold, who watched it with interest:

Tym guessed that the creatures of the air and the creatures of the earth had few chances to meet.

A final burst of song brought a third arrival – the sulkie who had been Tym's rowing companion. The Dreamwalker waved a hand – and a pool appeared in the dry plain. The sulkie eyed it with suspicion. Then it looked up at the Dreamwalker and, with a fatalistic shrug, dived in.

"Greetings, friends. I am the Dreamwalker. I am the bringer of dreams. When you cry out in your dreams, it is I who hear you." Tym's companions exchanged glances. *"I have called you because there is one here who is a friend to you all, and who now needs your help."*

"Needs our help does he?" The sulkie blew bubbles. *"In deadly danger, I suppose? It was only to be expected."*

Feobold still looked puzzled. *"But where are we?"*

"In the realm of dreams. Here, anything I wish to be, is."

"But we're not really here, are we?" The Gnome Prince looked around. *"I'm asleep, in my own bed. And things you make here aren't real. Are they?"*

The Dreamwalker tilted its great head on one side. *"It depends what you mean by 'here'. It depends what you mean by 'real'."*

"Ah." Feobold nodded wisely and decided not to ask any more questions.

"We are all in this human's debt." The sylph hovered close to Tym. *"What is your need?"*

Taking a deep breath, Tym told them his story from the very beginning. As soon as he mentioned discovering the essences of Earth, Air and Water in Herbit's chimney, the company became agitated.

"*We know this wizard.*" The sulkie's voice was disapproving. "*He is a wash-out. Many years ago, he visited our realm. He made quite a splash. He pretended to adore a female of our kind. She flipped, and when she was head over fins in love with him, he persuaded her to give him a sample of the essence of Water. Then, with a cruel cry of 'There's plenty more fish in the sea,' he left her.*"

"*So he did with our kind.*" The sylph's wings whirred angrily. "*A sylph-maiden became besotted with him…*"

"*Excuse me…*" Tym, remembering his old master's mean appearance and sour personality, was thunderstruck. "*This is Herbit we're talking about?*"

"*He was younger then,*" said the sylph defensively, "*and to be honest, the girl was a bit of an airhead. He had her flying round in circles after him – her feet never touched the ground. The minute she gave him the essence of Air, he took off. She came down to earth with a bump.*" The sylph grimaced. "*Very messy.*"

"*He did the same with a gnome maid. She worshipped the ground he stood on. He promised her the earth, the worm. But he treated her like dirt. Once he had the essence of Earth, he cut the ground from under her feet. After that, she opened a mine that fell in. You might say she buried herself in her work.*" Feobold brushed away a tear.

"*I know it doesn't make what Herbit did any better,*" said Tym slowly, "*but he never had any benefit from what he stole. Perhaps he was afraid to use the essences, or perhaps he didn't know how. I think he probably hoped that they'd make him rich and powerful, but they didn't. He isn't young any more and I think he's miserable. Perhaps he's always felt guilty about stealing them and betraying your people's trust.*"

The sylph looked doubtful. "*Perhaps. But you see why we*

hesitate to place our most precious possession in the hands of humans." Tym hung his head, hope fading. "*But tell us,*" continued the sylph, hovering over the silent figure of Zamarind, "*the rest of your story.*"

Tym did so, leaving nothing out. When he had concluded his tale with the gift of the Cumhera and the failure of his Whizzard speed, there was silence.

"*We do not give the essence of our elements lightly,*" said the sulkie. The others nodded. "*I don't suppose it would do you any good if we did.*" The morose creature sighed. "*Yet, your service to our kind has been very great.*" Feobold and the sylph nodded again. Tym looked up with new hope. "*And, however you came by it, it was your use of our combined essences to give you great speed that allowed you to help us in our need. The people of the sea will grant what you ask.*"

"*And the people of the air,*" said the sylph.

"*And the people of the earth,*" confirmed Feobold. Then the gnome looked troubled again. "*But how do we get it to you, here?*"

"*You all know of the preparation of the essences?*" said the Dreamwalker. Sylph, sulkie and gnome nodded. "*Then dream of it.*"

"*It won't work, you may depend on it.*" But the Sulkie closed its eyes and lay floating on its back in its pool. The Dreamwalker created a cloud for the sylph, who lay on it as if sinking into a soft feather bed. Feobold simply lay on the ground and closed his eyes.

For a long time, as it seemed to Tym, nothing happened. Then came sound. And shortly after that, movement.

Across the desert waste came a column of gnomes, marching with a rolling gait to the beat of drums and the deep music of horns. They approached with a steady pace, their mattocks at port arms. They were led by Thugmug, who gave Tym an approving grin and a thumbs-up.

Flowing from the pool came an honour guard of sulkies, singing a wailing, doleful song. They arrowed through the water and leapt and spun above it in a beautiful and complex dance.

Finally, the sylphs arrived, flying in a seemingly endless close formation, spinning, diving and turning aerobatically around the huge figure of the Dreamwalker, their thrumming wings making music from the wind.

Then all was still and one creature of each kind came forward. Almost lost in wonder, Tym accepted the essence of Air from the sylphs, the essence of Water from the sulkies. Thugmug himself, a big grin cracking his habitually angry face, presented Tym with the essence of Earth.

Feobold gave Tym an apologetic look. "*I know: I've never seen him smile either. But after all,*" he said, "*it's only a dream.*"

The creatures of all three elements bowed to Tym, and to each other: then with a tramping of feet, a whirr of wings and a thunderous splashing, they departed and the barren waste was empty once more except for the Dreamwalker, the fading Zamarind, Tym and his friends.

"*These essences being freely given,*" said the sulkie, "*will sustain your speed for longer. Not long enough, I daresay, and their effect will fade in time. Whenever you have need of more, dream of us and you shall have what you need. It will probably be too late, but* live in hope, that's what I always say." It snuffled wetly.

"*Thank you,*" said Tym humbly. "*How can I repay you?*"

"*The debt is ours to pay.*" The sylph smiled gently. "*Yet we would be glad to see the Whizzard and his companion in our realm. Perhaps one day, you will have a message to bear to the sylphs.*"

"*And to the sulkies.*"

"*And to the gnomes. Farewell, Whizzard.*"

Feobold waved and faded from view. The sulkie slapped the water with its fin-like feet and dived. The pool vanished. The sylph did a victory roll and spiralled up into the starless sky until it was lost to view.

The Dreamwalker scooped up the three phials containing the essences of the elements of Air, Earth and Water. Then there was a drumming of hooves on the barren earth and the Cumhera appeared, racing towards them. It halted and bowed daintily to Tym. Turning to the Dreamwalker, it breathed a great gout of flame. Tym gave a cry as the Dreamwalker's hands, clutching the precious essences, were bathed in Fire. But the great figure, undisturbed, turned its glowing eyes on Tym.

"*Go well,*" it said. "*And go quickly.*" Then the plain, the Cumhera, the Dreamwalker and the forlorn figure of Zamarind began to fade…

…And Tym awoke. It was dawn. The dream had ended. But beside him lay two freshly brewed bottles of Whizzard potion, glinting in the first rays of the rising sun.

Chapter Twenty-Three

How Tym and Colyn Walked On Water and What Befell the High Lord's Granddaughter.

Colyn drained the last drops of potion from his bottle and smacked his lips. "Not bad," he said, "but I'd prefer a spot of lemon with mine."

Tym let three drops of blood fall into his bottle of potion and then swigged the contents. He slipped the bottle inside his jerkin. "Right," he said, "let's go. We've still got to get the Cumhera scale back to Dun Indewood in time to save Zamarind."

Colyn looked at him. "How?"

"You've just had your potion, haven't you?" Tym stared at him. "What's the problem?"

"I 'esitate to bring this up," said Colyn cuttingly, "but we're still on the wrong side of the sea."

Tym stared at him, aghast. How could he have forgotten? It didn't matter how fast they could move, they still couldn't cross the sea without a ship. Unless… "I wonder," he said slowly, "if we went at the fastest speed we could manage, do you suppose we could run across the sea so fast that we wouldn't sink?"

Colyn gaped. "Now you really 'ave gone mad…"

"Well, we won't know till we try." Tym gritted his teeth and put his head down. Arms and legs moving so fast they were no more than a blur, he ran straight out on to the water… and kept going! His furiously racing feet skimmed the surface, never landing for long enough to sink below it. Tym was exhilarated. They could cross the sea. He turned to Colyn and stopped. "See? It's easy, we… *glub!*"

"Two pieces of advice!" Colyn called as Tym thrashed about. "One – when you're running on water, don't stop. Two – don't swaller! I'm not feelin' strong enough ter give yer any more Artificial Recreation!"

Tym doggie-paddled back to the shore, coughed up a surprising amount of sea water and got his breath back. Then they set off and were soon lost in the exhilaration of the new experience.

Running on water was fun! They hurdled the short waves and ran up and down the long ones. They burst through spray, laughing. They sped past a school of dolphins, matching them leap for leap. On they ran, leaving behind them twin arrow shaped wakes of curving sheets of spray, wild waves and turbulent water.

When they reached the land and re-entered the Dark Forest, they kept going. By dusk that evening, they had passed well beyond the country of the gnomes. Nevertheless, they had learnt from their earlier experiences and set watches throughout the night, one of them always on the alert for any threat that might emerge from the brooding trees. Another day and a night, they sped on their way. By the next evening, without further adventure, they emerged from the eaves of the Forest. Before them stood the walls of Dun Indewood.

At Whizzard speed, Tym and Colyn passed unseen through the City gates just before they were closed for the night. They threaded their way through the motionless crowds making their way homewards and sped up the hill to the Castle. Scooting across its rickety drawbridge into the courtyard, they finally arrived at the Palace of the High Lords. Climbing the great stone stairs, they sped along hushed corridors until they reached the Lady Zamarind's rooms.

Zamarind was still propped up in bed, as if she had not moved since their departure. She looked paler, however, and seemed more dull and lifeless than before. Lord Robat sat by her bedside, with the Runemaster and Humfrey the Boggart. As Tym and Colyn slowed to normal speed, the High Lord was speaking.

"...Say what you like, my granddaughter cannot live another night – and no sign of those scoundrels you sent off on a wild goose chase. They have failed me, and so have you."

Tym cleared his throat. "Erm – not exactly, my Lord." The effect was instantaneous – and gratifying. Lord Robat and his companions spun round and stared at Tym and Colyn as if they had grown an extra head apiece.

The Runemaster was the first to recover. "So, thou art returned. And hast thou that for which thou wast sent?" It took Tym a moment or two to work this out: when he had done so, he reached inside his jerkin, took out the scale of the Cumhera and held it aloft.

Lord Robat's mouth opened and closed a few times, giving him the look of a particularly astonished fish, but then he cried, "A spellbinder! Someone find me a spellbinder, egad!"

"Righto, Yer Worship." Colyn knuckled his brow. "I'll nip off and bring you one toot sweet." He disappeared at Whizzard speed.

Lord Robat pointed a trembling finger at Tym. "If the potion from this cures me granddaughter, you shall have half my kingdom..." The Runemaster cleared his throat. "Oh, all right, all right! Whatever happened to tradition? Well, in any case, you shall have any boon within my power to grant."

Before Tym could reply, Colyn returned, and nodded quickly to Lord Robat. "'S'cuse me, Yer Highness," he said and went into a whispered consultation with Tym.

"I hate to be a gooshberry..." Humfrey's dry voice cut across the conversation. The boggart was scowling. "If it ishn't too much trouble, would you care to tell the resht of ush what'sh going on?"

Tym bowed hurriedly to the High Lord. "I'm sorry, my Lord. My friend here was just telling me that he has found a wizard for you, one experienced in the art of potions, and..."

He got no further. The sound of approaching boots and roars of fury echoed down the corridor outside. "Put me down, you ruffians!" a voice howled. "D'you know who you're dealing with? I shall brew a potion to turn your bones to hot spikes of steel within you, by this hand—"

Colyn grinned as two guards came in, dragging a struggling and very dishevelled prisoner. "Special delivery, guv. One wizard, marked perishable. Where d'you want it?" The guards withdrew, leaving Herbit the Potions Master standing blinking before the High Lord.

"Found 'im in the market place, sellin' bottles o' nerve tonic to mugs," said Colyn. "I thought he'd do, if yer not perticuler."

Tym spoke up. "My Lord, it was potions from my master's store, however unwillingly given, that enabled us to achieve our quest. It is fitting that Master Herbit should prepare the potion to cure your granddaughter."

Lord Robat looked doubtful; but after a moment's hesitation, he nodded. Tym gave the Cumhera scale to Herbit, who accepted it like a man in a trance. The Runemaster led him off to the Palace workshops. Colyn again whispered to Tym, who nodded and turned to Lord Robat.

"My Lord, you have granted me a boon. Let it be this. You have in your dungeons a number of thieves who were arrested when your granddaughter was struck down. I ask you to pardon them."

"Now, hold it right there, shonny!" Humfrey was outraged. "We're grateful to you for bringin' the shcale back, but let'sh be realishtic. There are limitsh!" The boggart bowed to Lord Robat. "My Lord, I've been after shome of theshe shcoundrelsh for a long time! The crime rate has halved since we put that bunch of banditsh behind barsh!"

Tym thought quickly. "Then, my Lord, give them a choice.

Either to stay in jail, and face whatever punishment you decide for them – or to serve the City."

"Serve the City?" Lord Robat frowned. "How?"

"By making the Dark Forest around Dun Indewood safe for travellers." Colyn looked horrifed as Tym went on, "They say, 'Set a thief to catch a thief.' Pardon any outlaws who pledge to serve you as wardens and rangers, upholding the Laws of the City on the roads and byways of the Forest."

The High Lord considered. "Very well," he said at last. "Let it be so. We will employ any of those taken who confess their crimes and repent of their sins. We shall swear them to our service. Each shall wear a copper badge to denote his office and they shall therefore go by the name of… badgers!"

"I bet they flippin' won't," muttered Colyn ungratefully under his breath. "Fanks a bundle. I can't wait until my ol' dad hears about this lot. 'E'll go spare. "

An hour passed. The Lady Zamarind's Nurse was tearing her handkerchief to pieces and breathing (when she remembered to breathe at all) in great gulping sobs of anxiety. The waiting was hard to bear. Suppose Herbit messed up the brewing of the potion? Suppose it didn't work? Tym and Colyn exchanged nervous glances. Lord Robat paced, mumbling to himself. Humfrey the Boggart tidied the room.

At length, the Runemaster and Herbit returned. The High Lord's advisor looked stern, and the Potions Master apprehensive. He was carrying a flask of potion which seemed to steam and sparkle in the candlelight, as if it contained the sparks of a bonfire dancing in restless motion. Herbit bowed to Lord Robat. "The potion."

"Get on with it, man!"

Everyone held their breath as the Runemaster supported the still, frail figure of the Lady Zamarind, and Herbit tilted the flask of potion to her lips…

… Zamarind coughed and shuddered. Her eyes flashed as life returned to them and she spoke. "Yeeeuuurgh! What is that stuff? It tastes like a footbath! Anyone got any wine?"

Lord Robat gave a cry of joy, the old Nurse had hysterics and Colyn punched the air in celebration. Even the Runemaster permitted himself a slight smile.

Tym, feeling as if his heart would burst with elation, sprang forward with a joyful cry. "Zamarind!"

Zamarind gave Tym a look that would have melted a fishmonger's slab. "That's Lady Zamarind to you, knave! Where do you get off, insolent rascal, addressing the High Lord's heir in such familiar fashion! And anyway, what were you thinking of, bursting into a girl's bedroom, throwing homicidal wildlife about the place like some sort of demented zoologist? Of all the addle-pated, irresponsible, half-witted…"

As Zamarind continued her tirade, eyes flashing. Tym's expression was that of someone who, while out picking daisies, had strayed into the wrong field and suddenly been struck by the horns of a charging bull in the seat of his pants. He gaped, speechless.

Humfrey grinned. "I guessh she'sh feeling better."

Eventually, Zamarind ran out of names to call Tym and submitted to the tearful ministrations of her Nurse (though still casting smouldering looks over the old woman's shoulder at the unfortunate Whizzard).

Lord Robat turned to Herbit. "You have played your part in this business, fellow. Name your reward."

"If you please, my Lord…" Tym shook himself and managed to get his mouth back into working order. "May I suggest, that, in recognition of his service, Wizard Herbit be restored to the Order of the Magic Rectangle and appointed Potions Master to the High Lord…?"

Herbit gazed at Tym in astonishment and dawning hope.

"…Provided," Tym went on, "that he first visits the gnomes, the sylphs and the sulkies, and makes amends to them for his past misdeeds."

Herbit's face fell. "But that will take years," he protested.

"Then you had better get going," said the Runemaster.

Herbit shrugged fatalistically, but the look he gave Tym held little promise that he would ever regard his former apprentice as a friend.

"And what of yourself?" Lord Robat gave Tym an appraising look. "Technically, your life is forefeit. You have attempted to steal from my palace and endangered the life of the Lady Zamarind, all while under sentence of banishment."

Tym's heart sank. "My Lord, I ask nothing for myself."

"Do you not?" The High Lord stroked his chin thoughtfully. "Then I shall release you and your companion into the care of Humfrey here, for this night. We shall consider your fate. You shall know of our decision tomorrow."

CHAPTER TWENTY-FOUR

How Tym took a Fast Track to a New Career,
bringing this Tale to a Speedy Conclusion.

That night, Tym found himself once more in the realm of the Dreamwalker. He bowed to the great shadowy figure. *"Thank you, Master,"* he said formally. *"You have saved me from my folly and the Lady Zamarind from the consequences of it. I am in your debt."*

"In debt to your dreams?" The Dreamwalker sounded amused. *"I do not see how that can be. Yet you called me 'Master'."*

Tym nodded. *"I've been thinking about all that has happened. Your telling me how to make the potion, and my quest, and meeting the gnomes and the sylphs and the sulkies – and the Cumhera. I don't think all of that happened by accident."*

"*No.*" The Dreamwalker's eyes blazed for a moment. "*Though, in your foolishness, you made things as difficult for me as you could.*"

"I know," said Tym. "*Yet I have learnt a lot, as you intended I should.*"

The Dreamwalker nodded approvingly. "*And as you have learnt, so have you grown. You are no longer the wastrel you were.*"

"*No.*" For a moment, Tym felt a momentary pang of regret for those carefree days when he had shirked his responsibilities and hidden in the straw of his mother's barn.

"*You have learned of the people of Earth, Air, Water – and the creature of Fire, who perhaps taught you more than all. You have learned the value of each element. You have braved the dangers of the Dark Forest. You are ready for the task I have prepared you for: If the High Lord spares you, and if you choose to accept it.*"

"*And what is this task, Master?*"

"*What need you to ask? You know already.*" The Dreamwalker gestured, and a series of images formed before Tym's sleeping mind.

The Whizzard watched – and understood. "*Yes,*" he said slowly. "*Yes, I do…*"

Next morning, in the Great Council Chamber of Dun Indewood, Tym and Colyn (still in the custody of Humfrey the Boggart) appeared before Lord Robat and the Lady Zamarind. Luigi came with them. Strictly speaking, he had no business there, but he'd put Tym and Colyn up for the night at Humfrey's request and had tagged along as 'prisoners' escort'. Captain Gorge and Big Jim were brought up from the castle dungeons. Sundry guards were stationed around the room, more for show than anything else. The Runemaster, who sat in his accustomed place just below the High Lord, was the first to speak.

"Lord Robat has pondered long and hand upon just and fitting punishment for those malefactors e'en now before us," he said gravely.

Colyn nudged Tym. "Wot's 'e mean?"

Tym's face was haggard. "I think he means Lord Robat's going to throw the book at us." He glanced at the Lady Zamarind, who returned his look as if he was something she'd found wriggling in her salad.

"But first," the old wizard continued, "we shall hear the full story of the quest by which the scale of the Cumhera was secured and the Lady Zamarind's recovery assured." He stared straight at Tym who, with a sinking heart, stood and began his tale for what felt like the umpteenth time, starting at the moment he and Colyn had entered the Dark Forest.

When Tym reached their capture by the pirates, he hesitated, and bowed to the Runemaster. "My Lord, this part of my tale bears news for Captain Gorge."

The Runemaster nodded. "Captain Gorge, step forward."

The old pirate stood up. Tym continued the tale of his dealings with the Pirate Queen. Gorge listened with rapt attention as Tym told of the Sirens and the shipwreck.

"And so Captain Leysa went over the side," he said to

Gorge. "She would not let go her treasure and its weight pulled her down. She was drowned."

Captain Gorge sighed gustily. "My sweet little Leysa – gone! Still, she was a bully game bawcock to the end. Begotten in the galley and born under a gun. Every hair a rope yarn, every tooth a marline spike, every finger a fishhook and her blood right good caulking tar. May she sail into the sunset on starboard tack till her barque comes safe to harbour." The old seadog blew his nose and wiped his eyes.

The Runemaster raised his voice. "Captain Gorge, thou art a rogue. But for that thou didst lead us to knowledge of the whereabouts of the Cumhera, thou art pardoned."

"On condition," growled Lord Robat, "that if you must sing sea shanties, you do it somewhere deep in the Forest. If I have to listen to one more rousing ditty such as has been floating up from my dungeon this past week, I'll have you boiled in oil."

Captain Gorge waved a hand feebly. "Aye aye, Admiral," he said and slouched out, snuffling nostalgically.

Tym continued his story. At its conclusion, there was a silence. The Runemaster directed an inquiring glance at Lord Robat, who nodded.

"Big Jim, step forward." The Runemaster gave the brownie a stern look. "Hast thou been acquainted with the terms of the pardon the High Lord hath proposed?"

"Aye, and it's a diabolical bloomin' liberty," complained Big Jim in disgruntled tones. "Naked authoritarianism an' repression, that's what it is, a clear case of undemocratic totalitarian suppression of the justified grievances of the proletariat. But come the revolution, them as oppresses downtrodden thieves will be put against the wall and 'ave their weasands slit."

Tym raised his hand. "Ah – could you just tell me, while we're on the subject – what *is* a weasand?"

With a ferocious grin, Big Jim drew a grimy finger across his throat.

"Wot – right up there?" Colyn was scandalised. "I can't reach that high! I suppose I'll just 'ave to stick to cuttin' purses an' leave weasands alone."

"Will you take the proposal to the King of Thieves?" demanded the Runemaster, sharply. "Yes or no?"

"Aye, all right." Big Jim gave a grudging nod, still muttering under his breath, "But come the revolution…"

At a signal from Lord Robat, guards led Big Jim out. Colyn bit his fingernails and shook his head. "My old dad's not gonna like this. Not one bit, he ain't."

The Runemaster turned to Tym and Colyn. "It only remains to decide the fate of the Whizzard and his companion."

Luigi looked at the Runemaster's stern expression and bit his lip. "O boys, o boys, this don' look good. Sorry, my fren', I think you' right in the bolognese this time…" The pastafarian shook his dreadlocks sadly.

"For as much," said the Runemaster, "as they did cause the injury to the Lady Zamarind in the first place, in the course of a wicked plot to steal an heirloom of the House of the High Lords, both the prisoners are hereby sentenced to death…"

Tym bowed his head, Colyn groaned.

"However," the Runemaster continued, "in view of their valorous quest to the land of the Cumhera and successful return, and in view of a plea for clemency from the victim herself…" (Tym shot a startled glance at Zamarind, who gave him a quick smile before remembering herself and resuming her haughty stare) "…the execution of their sentence shall be postponed indefinitely, provided…" Here the Runemaster glanced at Zamarind and said in rather sour tones, as though repeating something he disagreed with: "Provided they are very sorry and promise not to do it again."

The next few minutes were rather confused. Luigi, beside himself with glee, hugged Tym and Colyn, kissing them repeatedly on both cheeks: Zamarind favoured them with a wintry smile. Humfrey grinned. "Don't supposhe we could catch you to shtring you up anyway," he confided, shaking Tym's hand. Tym and Colyn were graciously allowed to kiss Lord Robat's fingers as token of their pardon, before the High Lord and Zamarind (still darting looks at Tym over her shoulder) withdrew, signalling that the Council was at an end.

"Well, she came froo fer yer in the end, din' she?" Colyn grinned at Tym. "Good ol' Zammy. Yer want to push that along, sunshine."

Tym shook his head. "She didn't want me to be hanged. She felt sorry for me. That's all."

"I wouldn't be too sure." Colyn sighed. "I'd better go an' see 'ow me ol' dad's takin' the news that if 'is lads wants ter keep their 'eads out of a noose, they'll soon be wearin' badges on their chests." He looked round carefully and lowered his voice to a confidential murmur. "'Course, 'ooever the law is, they'd never stand a chance if you decided ter frow yer lot in wiv us. 'Ow's about it? Life o' freedom in the greenwood, unlimited archery practice, loads o'lolly an' all the venison yer can eat. My dose of potion'll wear off in a few days, but you can get as much as you want fer the askin'! An' wiv your speed an' my brains, we'd clean up."

Tym gave him a wry grin. "Thanks, but… I don't think I'm really cut out to be a thief."

"Suit yerself." Colyn seemed not the least abashed by Tym's refusal. "Be seein' yer…" He gave Tym an outrageous wink. "Some o' the time, at any rate." With a jaunty wave, Colyn sauntered from the Council Chamber.

Humfrey took Tym by the arm. "Decided what you're gonna do next?" the boggart demanded. Wondering, Tym shook his head. "You might like to conshider a position with Boggart and Rune," continued Humfrey, watching Tym closely. "Chief Roving Inqueshtigator, External Affairs. Whaddaya shay?"

"An Inquestigator? Nay." The Runemaster gave the boggart a disapproving look. He turned to Tym. "Thou woulds't have been a wizard once, lad," he said. "Is't still thy ambition?"

Tym felt he was drowning in a sea of opportunity. "I d-d-don't know," he stammered.

"Then consider on't. I have influence with the wizards of Dun Indewood. I can have thee apprenticed to the one of thy choice, if that is thy wish."

"You don' wanna go messin' with that wizard stuff!" Luigi had materialised at Tym's elbow. Ignoring the Runemaster's look of annoyance, the pastafarian went on, "I could use some 'elp in the restaurant. 'Ows about it? With your speed, you could clear the tables before the cust'mers knew they'd finished, an' do the washin' up before they got out the door!"

Tym looked from Luigi to Humfrey and the Runemaster. "Thank you for your kind offers, but I'm afraid I must refuse all of them."

The Runemaster looked disapproving. "If thou wouldst return to a life of idleness...."

Tym shook his head. "You misunderstand me. I told you that Colyn and I were guided on our quest by the Dreamwalker. It was he who first taught me to make the potion by which I became a Whizzard. My first duty is to the Dreamwalker, and he has a task for me."

His listeners looked at Tym with speculation as he went on: "For many years, Dun Indewood has had no contact with any other city. Yet the Dreamwalker told me that, before the Dark Forest spread to cover the land and prevent travel between them, there were many cities. According to the Dreamwalker, some of these still exist." Tym raised his voice. "This is the task for which the Dreamwalker has prepared me: to be a messenger between the scattered cities and realms of the Dark Forest, and between them and the other peoples that share our world, so that in time, we may know our neighbours better, and the Dark Forest may be less dark."

There was a long pause. Then Luigi said, "I's a pity. What a waiter you would have made—" He broke off. From outside the palace came a howling and a scrabbling sound, as of creatures with great paws scampering along stone-flagged corridors...

Tym had just time to cry, "The wish hounds" before the chamber doors burst open and he was smothered by invisible hairy bodies and his face licked by invisible rough tongues. The phantom dogs had indeed returned.

When Humfrey had at last succeeded in calling the hounds to order, he gave an exclamation. "Shay, bossh, thish one has shomething on it'sh back. Feelsh like shome short of shaddlebag… jusht a minute…" Humfrey fiddled with invisible clasps, grunting, and dipped his hand into a bag no one could see. The hand came out again bearing a scroll. Humfrey read the inscription, lips moving. Then with a curt, "It'sh for you," he handed it to the Runemaster, who broke the seal and read the contents.

He raised his head and said, "I think you should all hear this. It is a message from Will and Rose." Quelling the exclamations with an upraised hand, the Runemaster read,

Dear Roonmaster,

Hope you are well. Beste wisshes to Humfrey and Luigi. Greetings to Lord Robat.

Hav Tym and Colyn got back yet? If they hav, they may be intrested too no that, soon after we lefte them, we founde a city. It is called Dinas Ruined. The people have a pretty hard lyfe, but they were very interested to here there was another city, viz ours, and they greet His Lordship Robat FitzBadly and ~~rekwes reekwis riquis~~ ask hym to send a messinger to comense frootful contact between our cities. If Tym isn't too busy at the moment wood he fancie the job? We're sending this note with the wish hounds as they make the peeple of this city nervous, also they moult all over the carpet.

RSVP. All the best,

Will and Rose.

The Runemaster rolled up the scroll and looked quizzically at Tym. "Will you accept this task?"

Tym bowed. "Yes, my Lord. I shall carry messages for you and the High Lord, as quickly as I may, wherever you will have them sent."

Humfrey gave Tym a rueful grin. "Pity. You'd have made a darned good Inqueshtigator."

"Or maybe even," said the Runemaster drily, "by and by, a passable wizard."

"Perhaps," said Tym seriously. "But I think I'm doing the right thing. After all, there are plenty of wizards in Dun Indewood…"

He gave a grin – and disappeared. Moments later, his voice came faintly to their ears, echoing through the corridors of the ancient Castle.

"…But there's only one Whizzard!"

Forest River

Tym &
fa...

Mulch
Hemlock

Thieves
Hideout

Great
North
Road

Leafy Bottom

Laughing H...

Herbit's
Workshop

Dun
Indewood

Map of Tym & Colyn's Journey to the Land of the Cumhera

Desert

Island of the Sirens

Ship Wrecked

The Cumhera

Desert

nansland

The Pirates

The Sea

en Gate
dge

The Country of
the Gnomes

Order Form

To order direct from the publishers, just make a list of the titles you want and fill in the form below:

Name ....

Address ....

....

....

Send to: Dept 6, HarperCollins Publishers Ltd, Westerhill Road, Bishopbriggs, Glasgow G64 2QT.

Please enclose a cheque or postal order to the value of the cover price, plus:

UK & BFPO: Add £1.00 for the first book, and 25p per copy for each additional book ordered.

Overseas and Eire: Add £2.95 service charge. Books will be sent by surface mail but quotes for airmail despatch will be given on request.

A 24-hour telephone ordering service is available to holders of Visa, MasterCard, Amex or Switch cards on 0141- 772 2281.

An imprint of HarperCollins*Publishers*